Volume 1

D0826982

Volume I

by James Preller

SCHOLASTIC INC.

New York Toronto London Auckland Sydney
Mexico City New Delhi Hong Kong Buenos Aires

A Jigsaw Jones Mystery #1: The Case of Hermie the Missing Hamster,
ISBN 0-590-69125-2, Text copyright © 1998 by James Preller.
Illustrations copyright © 1998 by R. W. Alley.; *A Jigsaw Jones Mystery
#4: The Case of the Spooky Sleepover,* ISBN 0-590-69129-5, Text
copyright © 1999 by James Preller. Illustrations copyright © 1999 by
Scholastic Inc. Book design by Dawn Adelman.; *A Jigsaw Jones
Mystery #5: The Case of the Stolen Baseball Cards,* ISBN
0-439-08083-5, Text copyright © 1999 by James Preller.
Interior illustrations copyright © 1999 by Scholastic Inc. Book design
by Dawn Adelman.; *A Jigsaw Jones Mystery #6: The Case of the
Mummy Mystery,* ISBN 0-439-08094-0, Text copyright © 1999 by
James Preller. Interior illustrations copyright © 1999 by Scholastic Inc.
Book design by Dawn Adelman.

12 11 10 9 8 7 6 5 4 3 2 1   4 5 6 7 8 9/0

Printed in the U.S.A.   40

This edition created exclusively for Barnes & Noble, Inc.

2004 Barnes & Noble Books

ISBN 0-7607-5825-5

First compilation printing, June 2004

Contents

The Case of Hermie the Missing Hamster

For
Lisa

CONTENTS

Chapter One

Jigsaw Jones, Private Eye

It was Sunday afternoon, 4:36 P.M. I was in my office on the dirty side of town. Okay, actually I was in my tree house in the backyard. But it had a wooden sign that read OFFICE.

And it *was* dirty. But that's no big deal. When you're in my line of work, you get used to a little dirt.

No, I don't make mud cakes for a living. I'm a detective. For a dollar a day, I make problems go away.

I was working on my new "Life in the

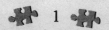

Jurassic" jigsaw puzzle. It wasn't going great. Okay, it was going crummy. My dog, Rags, yapped below. I told him to be quiet. Rags kept on barking. It was one of those days.

Suddenly a voice called out, "Hey, Jigsaw, you up there?" My next-door neighbor, Wingnut O'Brien, climbed the tree house ladder. His real name was Timothy, but everyone called him Wingnut because of his ears. They were three sizes too big for his head.

Wingnut didn't mind his nickname. In fact, he liked it. Wingnut was proud of his oversize ears. They made him feel special. Go figure. I thought they made him look . . . well . . . like a wing nut.

"What are you up to?" Wingnut asked.

"Oh, about ten feet," I answered.

Wingnut looked down. "Uh, yeah," he said.

Wingnut was six years old, a year

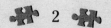

younger than me. He wore blue jeans, a hockey jersey, and a frown.

"Listen, Jigsaw, I've got a problem," Wingnut said.

"I make problems go away," I answered. "But it'll cost you. You know my rate: I get a dollar a day."

Wingnut's eyes started to water. Oh, brother. I handed him a box of Kleenex. In this line of work, you see a lot of tears. It pays to keep Kleenex around — especially if you don't have the stomach to watch somebody slobber all over his new hockey jersey.

Wingnut looked at me with sad, pitiful eyes. Between sobs and sighs, he sputtered, "Hermie's gone."

Hermie was Wingnut's golden hamster. It looked like this might be a job for Jigsaw Jones. Business had been slow and I needed the cash. Puzzles don't grow on trees, you know.

See, I've been solving problems in my neighborhood — and at school — ever since kindergarten. I was in second grade now, in Ms. Gleason's class. But some things never change. There are always problems — missing cupcakes, stolen baseball mitts, lost hamsters.

There will always be a need for me: Jigsaw Jones, Private Eye.

Chapter Two

A Slithery Suspect

I nodded toward an empty glass jar. Wingnut dug into his pockets. He dropped in two quarters, two dimes, a rubber band, and five nickels.

"You're a nickel short," I pointed out.

Wingnut's face got all squinched up. Like he was going to cry or something. "You can owe me," I said.

I took out my detective journal. It was a big, fat notebook. I never left home without it. I turned to a clean page and wrote the following words:

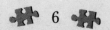

Underneath, I made two neat rows. On the top of one, I wrote Suspects. On the other, Clues. I underlined both words. Then I took out my colored markers and drew a picture of a hamster. Ugh. It looked like a rock with eyes and a tail.

Wingnut waited. I told him that this looked like a tricky case. "Before we go any further," I said, "let me call my partner. Wait here."

I ran into the house and called Mila. Luckily she was home. "Meet me at the office," I told her. "We've got a case."

"Don't forget to put Rags inside," Mila reminded me. Mila was allergic to Rags. Anything with fur made her sneeze. So she tried to stay away from cats and dogs.

Mila lived around the corner, and we'd been friends since we were in diapers. Mila worked with me on all the big cases. I paid her fifty cents a day. Mila demanded equal pay for equal work. It was a lot of money — but she was worth every cent.

Mila was over in ten minutes. When Mila climbed up the ladder, she was humming "The Short Vowel Song." We learned it in Ms. Gleason's class last week.

Mila sang:

"Where is short a? *Where is short* a?
Here I am. Here I am.
I am in a hat rack,
Cracker Jacks, and fat cats;
'a' • 'a' • 'a,' 'a' • 'a' • 'a.'

"Where is short e? *Where is short* e?
Here I am. Here I am.
I am in a red bed,
jelly eggs, and jet sets;
'e' • 'e' • 'e,' 'e' • 'e' • 'e.' "

If Mila wasn't humming something, she was probably singing. I didn't mind. She had a pretty voice.

We all sat together on the floor of the office. I poured lemonade and told Mila about the missing hamster.

Mila was all business. "When did you see Hermie last?" she asked Wingnut.

"Yesterday morning," Wingnut sniffled. "He was in his cage with Sammy — that's

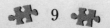

my other hamster — happily gnawing on a piece of cardboard."

"How did you know he was happy?" I asked.

Wingnut shrugged. "I dunno. He just had a happy face, I guess."

"Show me," I said.

Wingnut was confused. "Does it matter?"

"Everything matters," I said. "A mystery is like a jigsaw puzzle. You can't put it together until you have all the pieces. Show me," I repeated. "What *exactly* did Hermie look like yesterday morning?"

Wingnut half closed his eyes. He puffed out his cheeks. He tightened his lips and poked out his two front teeth. I had to admit it: Wingnut looked like a happy hamster. Okay, a happy hamster . . . with really big ears.

"Thanks, Wingnut," I said. "You never know. That may be the missing piece we need to solve the mystery."

Mila twisted her long black hair and sighed. She asked Wingnut, "Did Hermie have any enemies?"

Wingnut thought for a moment. "No," he said. "Everybody loves Hermie, even Jake, and he's a teenager. Most teenagers don't like *anything*."

Jake, better known as "Jake the Snake," was Wingnut's big brother. He was fourteen years old and a little strange. People called him "Jake the Snake" because he loved snakes. I mean, this guy *really* loved snakes. He had snake books, snake T-shirts, snake posters. But most important of all, he had a pet snake. A rosy boa. It was pretty big. Sometimes Jake brought it outside, wrapped around his shoulders. It was long, smooth, and totally gross. To be honest, I didn't really like snakes. Not even from a distance.

Under the word "suspects" I wrote Jake.

In the beginning of a mystery, everyone is a suspect. And *anything* is possible.

"Think hard," I told Wingnut. "Would anyone, or anything, want to harm Hermie?"

Wingnut shrugged his shoulders. "Well, I guess an owl would love to get at Hermie. He'd make a nice meal."

"Disgusting," Mila said.

"Any other enemies?" I asked.

"A cat, maybe," Wingnut said. Then he thought some more. "A snake . . . a . . . "

Mila sat bolt upright. "Did you say *snake*?"

Wingnut got all worried looking. "You don't think . . . ?"

"Jake's snake is only a suspect," I told Wingnut. "We'll need to come over to your house and look for clues."

"Uh, okay. But it's almost dinnertime. I can't have friends over on school nights."

"Sure, Wingnut." I patted him on the back. "Maybe tomorrow after school. Don't worry, pal. We'll find Hermie."

Wingnut left us alone in the office. "What do you think?" I asked Mila.

"I think," she said, "that we need to do some research."

"About hamsters?" I asked.

"Yes," she said. "And about the eating habits of snakes."

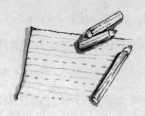

Chapter Three

A Matter of Life and Death

On Monday morning I was standing in the rain under a bright pink umbrella. Don't laugh. I couldn't find my Batman umbrella, so I had to borrow my sister's pink one. It even had flowers on it. Yeesh. I'd rather get wet. Everybody knows tough guys hate pink.

But those are the breaks when you're the youngest. I've got three older brothers and an older sister. People say it's easy being the youngest in the family. Well, I've got news for you. People are wrong. If you're the youngest, you get bossed around. You never win a fight. Your brothers call you "Worm" and "Shorty." And your parents make you wear baggy hand-me-down clothes — and borrow your sister's pink umbrella.

At school, I sat in Ms. Gleason's class, Room 201. There were sixteen kids in our class, including Mila. It was an okay day — for a Monday. During science we learned about the seashore. And for social studies we studied Christopher Columbus.

Monday was also an art day. I got to draw whatever I wanted. It came out pretty good:

Mila and I got our chance right before lunch. It was time for desk work. Ms. Gleason was grading papers. We walked up to her desk.

"Ms. Gleason," I said.

Ms. Gleason looked up and smiled. "Yes, what can I do for you two?"

"We really, really need to learn about snakes and hamsters," I said.

Ms. Gleason put down her blue pencil. "This sounds serious."

"It is," Mila answered.

"Very serious," I whispered. "It's a matter of life and death."

Ms. Gleason put her hand over her mouth. Her eyes got wide. "Oh, goodness," she said.

"Can you help us?" I asked.

"Well, I'll certainly try," she replied.

Ms. Gleason looked at the wall clock. In her loud teacher voice she said, "Class, lunch is in two minutes. Please put away

your projects and line up along the wall." She looked at Charlie Maloney goofing around with Mike Radcliff. Ms. Gleason suddenly looked tired. She pushed her hair away from her face. "Without killing each other," she added.

Ms. Gleason turned back to us. "Well," she said, "I can think of a number of ways you can find out about hamsters and snakes. How about you?"

"I thought of one," I said. "Asking you."

Ms. Gleason smiled. "That's a start, Theodore. How about you, Mila?"

Mila answered, "Well, you could look in a book or . . . maybe talk to somebody who knows a lot."

"Yeah," I said. "Like an expert."

"Excellent," Ms. Gleason said. "One of you can go to the library, either here at school or in town. I'm sure a librarian could help you find many wonderful books.

You might also want to visit the computer room and try searching the Internet."

"My mom can probably take me to the library after school," Mila said.

I frowned. "What about me?"

"Well, Theodore," Ms. Gleason said, "it looks like it's your job to find an expert."

Oh, brother. I always get the dirty work.

Chapter Four

World of Reptiles

Our plan was set. After school, Mila went to the town library to read about snakes. It was my job to visit a local pet store, World of Reptiles. We decided to meet back at my house in an hour. There was only one problem. I needed a ride. Fortunately, my sixteen-year-old brother Billy had just gotten his driver's license. He always jumps at the chance of borrowing my mom's car.

Screech! Billy slammed on the brakes in

front of the pet store. He told me he'd pick me up in ten minutes.

"Make it fifteen," I said.

"You got it, Jigsaw."

Billy was my favorite brother. He was the only one who called me Jigsaw. My brothers Daniel and Nicholas were tied for second place. My sister, Hillary, came in last. I know it wasn't her fault, but I was still unhappy about the umbrella.

World of Reptiles was a dark, stuffy little store. There was one customer inside. He was a skinny man with a leather jacket and black boots.

Behind a counter sat a dark-haired woman. She smiled at me. She had a snake tattoo on her right arm. "Can I help you?" she asked.

"Just looking," I said.

Reptile tanks and cages lined the walls. This store had every kind of weird animal you could imagine. It had skinks, ferrets,

Gila monsters, box turtles, and talking parrots — even monkeys wearing diapers.

It also had snakes. Lots of snakes. Small skinny ones — and very, very big ones.

I stopped in front of the biggest cage. It was glass, about ten feet tall. Inside there was a yellow python thicker than my leg. It was curled up in a corner. It must have been thirty feet long.

"What does he eat?" I asked the lady.

She pointed to a large metal cage. I looked. It was filled with rabbits.

"He eats . . . bunnies?" I asked.

She nodded. I glanced at the cage again. Poor little fuzz balls.

Another customer went up to the counter. "I'll take six mice," he ordered.

After he left, I went up to the woman. "I didn't know people kept mice as pets," I said.

"Oh, no," she answered. "They aren't pets. The mice are food. Snake food."

I gulped. "Would a snake eat a hamster?"

She explained, "A snake would *love* to eat a hamster. But people buy the white mice instead. They're cheaper."

She came around the counter and led me to a cage. Inside were two rosy boas.

"Two weeks ago," she said, pointing at a tan snake with a reddish tip on its tail, "this slippery rascal got out. In the morning, I found him on top of the hamster cage."

"Did he eat the hamsters?" I asked.

She shook her head. "No, they were safe. The hamster lid was on tight." She pushed the wire roof. It didn't budge an inch.

"Can hamsters escape?" I asked.

"Sure," she said. "But only if the lid isn't on tight enough."

"But how do they get out?" I asked. "Can they climb glass walls like Spider-Man?"

"No," she said with a laugh. "They jump

and hang onto the edge. Actually, it's pretty amazing."

I thanked the nice woman and headed for the door. I'd seen enough snakes to last a lifetime.

Chapter Five

Bad News for Hermie

Back home, I sat down to eat a Popsicle. It made me feel better. This case was getting complicated. Things were not looking great for Hermie.

Plus I couldn't stop thinking about those rabbits. Somehow eating a mouse seemed okay. But a bunny — oh, brother. Just the thought of it made my stomach hurt.

Where was Mila? She should have been back by now. But if you put a book in front of Mila, she might never look up.

Suddenly I heard a voice.

 27

"Earth to Theodore, Earth to Theodore. Can you hear me?"

"MOM!" I cried. "I am NOT Theodore. I'm Jigsaw, Jigsaw Jones. And I'm working on a Very Important Case."

"I see," my mom answered. "Well, Mr. Jigsaw Jones," she said. "How about working on that room of yours? It's a disaster."

"Can't," I explained. "Things to do, mysteries to solve."

My mom put her hands on her hips. "Maybe I'm not being clear," she said. "I wasn't *asking*, I was *telling*. And now I'm *exclaiming*: Clean your room — now!"

So. She wanted to play tough.

I decided to hide out in my room for a while. Sorry, but cleaning a room was no job for the world's greatest second-grade detective. Somewhere out there a little hamster was depending on me. A little furry guy without a friend in the world. Maybe he was lost. Maybe he was stolen. Maybe he was lunch.

This was no time for putting away Legos.

I pulled out my detective journal and reviewed the facts of the case. I listed all the key words:

Hermie, Wingnut, Mystery, Missing, Boa, Python, World of Reptiles, and Jake.

I put the words in ABC order. It wasn't easy. Ms. Gleason said I needed to practice my ABC order. My list looked like this:

Boa
Hermie
Jake
Missing
Mystery
Python
Wingnut
World of Reptiles

ABC order isn't that hard. Except I sometimes get mixed up with *M* and *N*. That's because whoever made up the alphabet got it all wrong. *N should* come first, then *M*. I mean, look at it this way. If you want to build an *M*, you start with an *N*. Then you just draw another line. But you can't draw an *M* without an *N* already waiting there. That's why I think the alphabet is inside out.

But try telling that to Ms. Gleason.

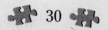

Bbbring! It was the doorbell.

"I'll get it!" I yelled. I raced to the door. It was Mila. She had three books in her arms.

And she looked worried.

Mila set the books down on our kitchen table. She wasn't humming. That meant bad news.

"I've been reading about snakes," she told me. "Look at what I found."

Mila opened a book to a picture of a snake. It had a mouse in its mouth. Correction: It had *half* a mouse in its mouth. The other half had already been swallowed.

"This snake is a rosy boa," Mila said. "The same kind of snake that Jake owns."

"Are they poisonous?" I asked.

"No, boas and pythons are in the constrictor family," Mila explained. She flipped through the pages of a book called *Killer Snakes*. Mila began reading out loud:

" 'Constrictors kill their prey by wrapping their bodies around them and squeezing. They squeeze until the victim stops breathing. They swallow their victims whole.' "

"Those constrictors remind me of my aunt Harriet," I told Mila. "My brother Billy calls her the Anaconda. When Aunt Harriet comes to visit, she can hug the life out of you."

I hugged myself and squeezed tight. Then I made all sorts of disgusting choking sounds. I fell on the floor, dead.

Mila didn't seem to notice.

We looked at more pictures. There was one of a snake swallowing an alligator. Then there was another picture of the same snake after it was done eating. It looked like a hat.

I took out my markers and drew a picture in my detective journal. It looked like this:

Mila said, "These snakes are giant pythons. They live in jungles in Africa and Asia. Jake's snake is a lot smaller."

I put my markers away. "Maybe Jake's snake is different. Maybe it doesn't eat mice. Maybe it just eats pizza. Or pretzels. Or something like that."

"Maybe," Mila said doubtfully. "But we still don't know if the snake had *opportunity*."

"Opportunity?" I asked.

"Yes, opportunity," Mila repeated. "We don't know if the snake could have gotten to Hermie's cage."

I stood up. "Then we'd better go," I said.

"Go?" she asked.

"Yes," I said. "Let's visit the scene of the crime."

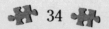

Chapter Six

Wingnut's Room

We had to ring the bell three times before Mrs. O'Brien answered the door. She had the handle of a big vacuum cleaner in her hand.

"Hello, Theodore. Hello, Mila." She smiled. "Have you been ringing long?" Mrs. O'Brien wiped her forehead with the back of her hand. "This new vacuum cleaner is so loud, I can't hear a thing."

Wingnut appeared at the door. We followed him into his room. It was spotless. "Sorry about the room," he apologized.

"My mom just bought a superpowerful vacuum cleaner. She's been cleaning for days. So don't leave anything lying around. She might suck it up!"

Yeesh. Wingnut's room gave me the creeps. It was clean, all right. *Too clean.* Everything was neat. Books were neatly on the shelves. Toys were neatly put away. Even the floor was neat. How can a guy live like that? It just wasn't normal.

Mila walked over to the hamster cage. It was on a low shelf, about knee-high.

One hamster lay curled up in the corner. "That's Sammy," Wingnut said. "He's sleeping. Hamsters mostly sleep all day. They like to run around at night."

"Ah-choo!" Mila sneezed.

"Bless you," I said.

The cage looked like a fish tank. Except it didn't have any water in it. And no fish. It

had a wire roof. Mila poked at it. The roof moved a little, but not much. I doubted that a hamster could get through a hole that small.

"Do you always keep the lid on?" I asked.

"Yes," Wingnut said. "I'm really careful about it. One night, after cleaning the cage, I forgot to put it back on. Hermie escaped. We didn't find him for two whole days."

Mila sneezed . . . and sneezed again.

I got tired of saying "Bless you" all the time. But like my dad says, "Having manners is a full-time job." Even if you have to say the same thing — over and over and over again.

I tried to imagine what it would be like to eat a hamster. Mila and Wingnut watched as I slithered on the ground. I flicked my tongue into the air. I looked at Sammy in the cage. Yuck! I was glad that I wasn't a snake. I'd rather eat pizza.

"Where is the snake?" Mila asked. She

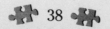

looked at me crawling on the floor. "The real one," she added.

"Across the hall," Wingnut answered. "In Jake's room."

"Can we see it?" she asked.

"Sure. I don't think Jake's home," Wingnut said.

"I don't know," I said. "Teenagers don't like people in their rooms."

"Aw, come on," Wingnut said. "It's no big deal."

Jake's door had a sign on it. It said:

THE SNAKE PIT!
DEATH TO ALL WHO ENTER!!!

Wingnut knocked. No one answered. Wingnut slowly pushed open the door.

We stepped inside. It was dark. And creepy. And it smelled like snake.

That's when Mila screamed.

Chapter Seven
Enter the Snake Pit

"EEEECK!"

I must have jumped about fifty million feet. Mila pointed at a stereo speaker. There it was — the rosy boa. Curled up in a ball. It looked calm and peaceful. The problem was, it wasn't in a cage. I felt a little wiggle in my stomach.

Wingnut said, "Don't be afraid. Jake lets him out of the cage all the time."

I stood behind Mila.

"He's harmless," Wingnut said. "Jake says that snakes are the most misunderstood creatures in the animal kingdom."

Wingnut petted the snake's smooth skin. "See? Snakes don't like to bother anybody."

"Tell that to a mouse," Mila muttered.

"Or a bunny," I added.

I looked around. Jake sure had a weird room. The lightbulbs were black. They gave off a strange light that made Mila's white shirt glow. He had posters all over the walls. Mostly basketball stars, snakes, and a goofy one of a bunch of dogs playing cards. Go figure.

Just then, the door flew open. It was Jake — and he looked mad. "What are you pip-squeaks doing in my room?" he roared. "Didn't you read the sign?"

I felt another wiggle in my stomach.

Wingnut stepped forward. "Sorry, Jake. It was an emergency." He pointed at me. "Jigsaw is a detective. He's trying to help me find Hermie."

Jake looked at me. "A pip-squeak detective, eh? Well, try again, Sherlock. You can bet Hermie's not in here. Or else Goliath would have gotten him."

Goliath, I guessed, was Jake's boa.

"Actually," I said, "I was wondering if Goliath had opportunity."

"Opportunity?" Jake asked.

"Yes," I said. "Could it have slithered into Wingnut's room?"

Jake shook his head. "No way, no how. Goliath doesn't leave this room unless I take him."

"Are you positive?" Mila asked.

"Sure I am," Jake said. "Besides, if he got out, I would have known about it. Or my mom would have seen him. She's been vacuuming everything in sight for days."

Jake picked up the snake. He brought him to Mila. "Here," Jake said, "touch him."

Mila touched Goliath. "He's not slimy at all," she said.

"How about you?" Jake said, bringing the snake to me.

"Er, no thanks," I said.

Jake brought the snake closer to my face. "Come on," he said.

Jake wasn't being very nice. After all, I didn't like snakes. My stomach jiggled and wiggled. I suddenly felt dizzy. Like I'd just eaten three hot dogs — and gone on a roller coaster about eight times in a row.

Like I was going to get sick or something.

And I did.

Right on Jake's Air Jordans.

Chapter Eight

Person, Place, or Thing

There was a knock on my bedroom door.

"I'm not here," I moaned.

My brother Billy walked in. "I heard about what happened. How are you feeling, tough guy?" he asked.

"Rotten," I said.

Billy put down a plate of buttered toast and a cup of honey tea on my night table. "Mom said you should try to eat something," he said.

"I'm never going to eat again," I said.

Billy sat on the edge of my bed. "Don't

take it so hard, Jigsaw. Everybody throws up."

"Not on somebody's sneakers," I said.

Billy smiled. "I wish I had been there to see Jake's face. He must have freaked."

I sort of laughed, too. It *was* pretty funny.

"How's the case going?" Billy asked.

"Rotten," I said. "There's no way Jake's boa could have done it. I'm ready to give up."

Billy put his hand on my shoulder. "You'll solve the mystery," he said. "Keep working at it."

After the toast and tea, my stomach felt a little better. But my heart still felt lousy. I was worried about Hermie. Where was he? Could someone have stolen him? Was he still alive?

I figured that working on a jigsaw puzzle might make me feel better. I had a new one that I hadn't opened yet. It was called "Monsters of Hollywood." I laid all the pieces on the floor. You can't start a puzzle until you've looked at every piece.

Jigsaws were like mysteries. . . .

"That's it!" I said. I grabbed my detective journal. Maybe I had missed a clue. I needed to look at all the pieces again.

In school we were learning about the parts of speech. I decided to do the same thing with the facts of the case. On top of one page, I wrote the word **PERSON**. On the next page, I wrote **PLACE**. On the one after that, I wrote **THING**.

Then I thought about everything that had to do with the case. And I mean *everything*.

My final lists looked like this:

PERSON	PLACE	THING
Wingnut	World of Reptiles	Hermie
Jake	My office	Sammy
Pet store owner	Wingnut's room	Goliath (Jake's snake)
Jigsaw (ME!)	Library	Vacuum cleaner
Mila	Jake's room	Vomit
Wingnut's mom	School (Room 201!)	Hamster cage
Ms. Gleason		

It was mostly pretty easy. I wasn't so sure about the **THING** column. I mean, I knew Hermie wasn't a person or a place. But he seemed like *more* than just a **THING**.

Looking at all the facts seemed to help. I thought about Wingnut . . . and Hermie . . .

and Jake . . . and World of Reptiles. Something was bothering me.

I closed my eyes and tried to remember my visit to the store.

I remembered the man buying the mice. I remembered the poor bunnies, the nice lady's tattoo, the hamster cage. Then it hit me. *KLUNK!* Like a baseball bat smashed on my head.

When the lady pushed the hamster roof, it didn't budge. But in Wingnut's room, the hamster roof was loose. Not very loose. Just a little.

Maybe that was enough.

Maybe Hermie had escaped after all!

He might still be alive. Then I began to worry. How long could a hamster survive without food?

I switched off the light and went back to bed. School tomorrow. It was going to be another busy day.

Chapter Nine
The Phony Clue

"Okay, class," Ms. Gleason said. "It's organization time. You know your jobs."

At last the school day was almost over. Now all we had to do was get ready for tomorrow. We had to clean up, sharpen our pencils, and get our coats. Plus some kids had special jobs at the end of the day. There were Board Cleaners and Book Checkers. Chair Putter-Uppers and Closet Neateners and Homework Checkers. The best job was Zookeeper. But our gerbil died a few weeks ago. So now we were the only second-grade class in the whole school without a pet. We didn't need a Zookeeper anymore.

I had a free day. So I neatened up my desk superfast.

I raised my hand. "Ms. Gleason," I said.

Ms. Gleason came over to my desk. "Thank you for raising your hand, Theodore," Ms. Gleason said. "And by the way," she whispered, "how's that matter of life and death coming along?"

"Not so great," I said. "I threw up on Jake O'Brien's sneakers yesterday."

"Oh," Ms. Gleason answered. "That's not fun." She moved back a step.

"And I have another problem." I told her that I needed to find a phone number.

"That's not a problem," she said.

"It is," I answered, "if you don't know how."

Ms. Gleason walked to her desk and

pulled out a big, fat phone book. She explained, "Phone books are in two parts, Theodore. The first part is called the white pages. It lists the phone numbers of all the people who live in our area." She flipped through the book. "This other section is called the yellow pages. See? The pages are yellow. It lists the phone numbers for all the businesses."

"Super," I said. "Could you tell me the phone number for World of Reptiles?"

Ms. Gleason smiled. "No," she said. "You'll have to look it up yourself." She handed me the book. "Everything is in alphabetical order," she said. "By category."

"Category?" I asked. This wasn't turning out so hot.

"Yes. What *kind* of business is World of Reptiles? Is it a restaurant? Do they serve lizard stew?" Ms. Gleason laughed at her joke.

I didn't laugh. I told Ms. Gleason that it was the name of the pet store.

"Then you can start by looking under *P*, for pets."

Oh, brother. Teachers. You try to get a simple answer and all you get is more work.

By the time I found the phone number, it was nearly time to go. I put on my jacket and lined up for the bell. I found a note inside my pocket. It was in code:

20–8–9–19∗9–19∗1∗6–1–11–5∗3–12–21–5.

I knew the note was from Mila. She was always testing my brainpower. I'd seen a code like this before. It was called a substitution code. All you had to do was write out the alphabet. Then you had to write the numbers one to twenty-six underneath each letter. They worked together in pairs. Each number in Mila's code stood for a letter. I solved it on the bus.

Then I scribbled a quick message to Mila. I figured that I'd put it on her desk tomorrow. It looked like this:

Chapter Ten

Another Fine Mess

I called World of Reptiles right after school. The pet store owner was very nice. She told me everything I needed to know. Then I raced over to Wingnut's house. There wasn't any time to lose.

"Is your mom home?" I asked Wingnut.

"Nope," Wingnut said. "She went food shopping."

"Good," I said. "Jake?"

"He's in his room." Loud music throbbed from behind Jake's door.

I hesitated. "Do you think it's safe?"

Wingnut nodded. "Jake said he never wants to be in the same room with you again."

"Fine with me," I said. "We have to work fast. I think I know where Hermie is."

Wingnut was thrilled — until I told him where. "I don't know, Jigsaw," he said. "My mom might get really mad. It's a brand-new vacuum cleaner."

I looked at him. "Do you want to find Hermie or not?"

Wingnut was still nervous. But he brought the vacuum cleaner into the living room anyway.

The clues had been in front of me all the time. The new vacuum cleaner . . . the superclean bedroom . . . the wobbly hamster lid.

I explained it again to Wingnut. "Listen, pal. It all makes sense." I leaned closer to him and whispered in his ear. "I just talked on the phone with the lady from World of

Reptiles. She told me that hamsters are really good squeezers. They can squeeze through the teeniest, tiniest holes. That lid of yours wasn't on tight enough," I said. "That's how Hermie escaped."

Wingnut was nervous. "But what does my mom's vacuum cleaner have to do with it?"

"Think, Wingnut. Jake said that your mom's been vacuuming everything in sight. There isn't a speck of dust in your room. That was a clue. I bet that your mom vacuumed in there — around the same time Hermie escaped."

Wingnut looked at the vacuum cleaner. "You don't think . . . ?"

I nodded. "Hermie's in there."

Opening up the vacuum cleaner wasn't easy. There were a few weird latches that I didn't understand. I tried prying it open with a screwdriver — but that didn't work.

"Have you got a hammer?" I asked.

A few good whacks did the job. Unfortunately, it did a little too good of a job. Part of the vacuum cleaner shattered, sending pieces of plastic flying through the air.

"Jigsaw!" Wingnut exclaimed. "Be careful!"

I looked at Wingnut. It seemed like he might start crying again. "Don't worry, pal," I said. "With a little tape, it will be as good as new."

I emptied the vacuum bag on the carpet. Dust flew everywhere. "We'll clean up this mess later," I said. "Let's start looking for Hermie."

We were finished in ten minutes. We found two toys from Wingnut's Star Wars collection — Chewbacca and R2-D2. We found six rubber bands and a paper clip. We found a purple crayon and half of a Ken Griffey baseball card. We even found hamster hair.

But we didn't find Hermie.

Unfortunately, Mrs. O'Brien found us — sitting on the rug, surrounded by dirt and dust and broken plastic. The vacuum cleaner was in pieces.

I can't really blame her for screaming.

Chapter Eleven
The Ah-choo Clue

We heard Mila coming even before she knocked. She was singing again:

"Where is short i? Where is short i?
Here I am. Here I am.
I am in a big fig,
Silly Rick, and pig wig;
'i' • 'i' • 'i,' 'i' • 'i' • 'i.'

"Where is short o? Where is short o?
Here I am. Here I am.
I am in a hot pot,

Rocky top, and stop clock;
'o' • 'o' • 'o,' 'o' • 'o' • 'o.' "

"Hey, guys." She saw our sad faces. "What's wrong?"

"I'm in big trouble," Wingnut said. "And it's all his fault."

"I said I was sorry about a million times already," I complained.

Mila looked around. "Hey, where's your hamster cage?"

"I'm keeping Sammy in my parents' room," Wingnut said. "I think he's safer there."

I didn't listen to them. I was trying to think. The snake didn't get Hermie. The vacuum cleaner didn't get Hermie. Where could he be?

Mila leaned against the closet door and sneezed. "Ah-choo!" Then she sneezed again.

I was in a rotten mood. "Mila," I snapped.

"Could you *please* stop sneezing? I'm trying to think."

Mila folded her arms. "I can't help it, Jigsaw. You know I'm allergic to fur. I always sneeze if I get too close to it."

"But there isn't any fur in my room," Wingnut said. "Hermie is gone and so is Sammy."

Mila sneezed again. "Well," she sniffled, "something is making me sneeze."

Mila and I looked at each other. We shouted at once: "HERMIE!"

The search was on!

Wingnut looked under the bed. I took the closet. Mila searched through the toy chest.

We didn't find a thing.

We were about to give up when I had an idea. A crazy idea. A wonderful, fantastic, crazy idea.

"Have you guys ever heard of metal detectors?" I asked.

Mila spoke up. "Sure, people use them to find old coins and stuff like that. If the detector comes near metal, it beeps."

"That's right," I said.

Mila shrugged. "So?"

"So . . . we've got a hamster detector right here. But instead of beeping, it sneezes," I answered. "It's you, Mila!"

It was worth a try. Mila slowly walked around the room. She didn't sneeze until she got near the closet. "Ah-choo!"

"Stop!" I yelled.

Mila sneezed again. She got down on her hands and knees. Then she really started sneezing like crazy.

Wingnut and I got down next to her. All three of us crawled into the closet. Mila put her nose next to a poster tube that was lying on the floor. She sneezed on it. Three times.

I looked inside.

I couldn't believe my eyes.

I patted Wingnut on the back. "Guess what, pal. We've found Hermie. But there's just one thing you should know," I said. "Hermie is a . . . SHE!"

Wingnut looked into the tube. He saw Hermie nestled inside the tube . . . feeding baby hamsters!

Wingnut was confused. "If Hermie is a she . . . " he said.

"Then Sammy is a daddy!" Mila added.

We left Wingnut alone in his room. He was happily cooing into the cardboard tube.

"Happy birthday, little guys," he gently whispered.

Chapter Twelve
Student of the Week!

A week later, I walked into World of Reptiles. I was singing a new song that I'd just made up:

"Where is Herm-ie? Where is Herm-ie?
Here I am. Here I am.
I am in a new cage,
loving all my babies.
Her–er–me. Her–er–me."

"Hello again," said the nice lady. "You seem happy today."

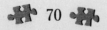

"Oh, I am," I said. "I'm very happy." I told her about the hamster babies. And I thanked her for all the help.

"So what brings you here?" she asked.

"Supplies," I said. "My teacher and I are cooking up a surprise for the whole class."

* * *

The school bell rang. But I waited outside the classroom door. It was part of the secret plan. I could hear Ms. Gleason talking to the class.

"Settle down, boys and girls," said Ms. Gleason. "As you know, Black Fang the gerbil died recently. It was a sad time for us all. But today Theodore and I have a special surprise for you."

Ms. Gleason opened the door. "Come in, Theodore."

I walked in, holding the surprise in my arms. No one could tell what I had because it was hidden under a sheet. I smiled at Mila — she was the only person who knew about the secret.

"Children," Ms. Gleason said, "I'd like you to meet our new class members — ta-da!" She pulled off the sheet.

I was holding a brand-new hamster cage. Inside, there were two baby hamsters — gifts from Wingnut O'Brien.

Everyone cheered and hooted.

"Theodore, please put our new friends on the back shelf."

Everyone watched as I walked to the back of the room.

Ms. Gleason said, "Class, I think Theodore deserves a big round of applause. Because it was all his idea."

The kids cheered again, even louder than before. I was proud. And so was Mila. It couldn't have happened without her help. Sure, she was still allergic to hamsters. But Mila said it wasn't a problem if she didn't

get too close to them. The only bad thing was, Mila could never be Zookeeper.

"One last thing," Ms. Gleason said. "I've decided to name Theodore Student of the Week."

She handed me a piece of paper with beautiful squiggly lines all around it. Ms. Gleason called it a certificate.

When I sat down at the table, everyone at my table wanted to look at it. Mila read it out loud:

STUDENT
of the
WEEK

Theodore Jones has been named Student of the Week because *he gave Room 201 two pet hamsters*. Thanks for helping to make our classroom a nicer place. I am so proud of you!

CONGRATULATIONS!

Ms. Gleason
Room 201

Mila put down the certificate and smiled.

I looked around. Everybody was smiling. Even Ms. Gleason.

Good old Wingnut, I thought. It was nice of him to give us those hamsters.

But now the case was closed. I needed a new mystery to solve. Somehow I knew there would be one. There always was.

Like I said before, I make problems go away. And there are always problems — missing cupcakes, stolen baseball mitts, lost hamsters . . .

There will always be a need for me: Jigsaw Jones, Private Eye.

The Case of the
Spooky Sleepover

For
Mike & Mary

CONTENTS

Chapter One

Ralphie Jordan

Ralphie Jordan was the most popular kid in room 201. Everybody liked Ralphie. And Ralphie liked everybody right back. He had dark eyes, dark skin, dark hair — and he was as thin as a flagpole. Best of all, Ralphie Jordan was a world-champion smiler. Nobody had a bigger smile or used it more often.

Only today, Ralphie wasn't smiling.

He plopped down next to me in the school cafeteria. "Hey, Jigsaw," he said. "Can I talk to you for a minute?"

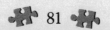

It's hard to talk with peanut butter in your mouth. I know. I've tried it. "Mmuffurf," I mumbled. I reached for my milk and swallowed hard. "Whew," I said. "That's better."

Ralphie flashed a toothy grin. But the smile left his face in a hurry, as if it had somewhere else to go. That wasn't a good sign. Something has to be wrong if Ralphie Jordan doesn't smile. "What's the matter?" I asked. "Bologna again?"

"Nah, nothing like that," Ralphie said. And as if to prove it, he poured out his lunch bag on the table. Then he lined up everything in a neat row. Ralphie had a ham sandwich, a plastic bag of grapes, two Oreo cookies, a carrot, and a juice box. He picked up the ham sandwich and squished it between his hands. By the time he was done, the sandwich was flatter than Flat Stanley. Ralphie took a few big bites of the sandwich, then twisted open an Oreo. He licked the white insides. "You're still a detective, right?" he asked.

"Sure," I answered. "For a dollar a day, I make problems go away."

Ralphie didn't say anything. He was busy working on his second Oreo. I waited. In the detective business, things go better when you sit back and listen. So that's what I did.

Finally Ralphie spoke up. "Can you keep a secret?" he whispered.

"I can," I said. "But when I'm on a case, I share the facts with Mila Yeh. We're partners, you know."

Ralphie thought that over. He shrugged. "I don't know. It's sort of goofy."

I waited for the goofy part to come.

It came.

"Jigsaw," Ralphie asked, "do you believe in ghosts?"

Chapter Two

On Top of Spaghetti

"Ghosts?" I repeated. "Like Casper the Friendly?"

Ralphie Jordan shook his head. "No, the *unfriendly* kind."

Maybe it was the look on his face. Maybe a window was open and a cold breeze blew down my back. But I got a creepy feeling. Like watching a scary movie with the lights out.

"Ghosts aren't real," I told him. The truth was, I didn't know for sure. But one thing was certain. I didn't want Ralphie Jordan to

think I was scared. No one needs a fraidy-cat detective.

Ralphie sort of frowned. Then he gave me a big, easy smile. A Ralphie Jordan Special. But I knew it was just an act.

"What's this about?" I asked. "You haven't seen a ghost, have you?"

"Forget it," Ralphie said. "It's probably nothing."

"Sure, probably nothing," I agreed. "But if you want to talk, I'll be in my tree house after school. Come by if you feel like it."

"Thanks, Jigsaw," Ralphie said. "I think I will." Then Ralphie pointed to his uneaten lunch — the carrot, grapes, and juice. "Want it?" he asked.

I didn't and I told him so. Ralphie stuffed his leftovers into his lunch bag. He crumpled the bag into a tight ball. Then he stood up, turned, and fired. The bag floated toward the garbage can.

Swish.

"Yes!" Ralphie called out in a fake announcer's voice. "Jordan shoots . . . and scores!"

After Ralphie left, I pulled out my detective journal. I ripped out a piece of paper and wrote a message to Mila. We wrote all our messages in code. I decided to use a space code. All I had to do was write out the message without putting spaces between the words. It looked like this:

MEETMEATTHETREEHOUSEAFTERSCHOOL.

I looked it over. Too easy, I decided. So I took out another piece of paper and tried again. I added spaces in the wrong places. Now it looked pretty tricky.

ME ETMEA TTHETRE EHOU SEAFTERSC HOOL.

Mila needed to find the real words and draw lines to separate them. When Mila was done, it should look like this:

ME ET/ ME/ A T/ THE/ TRE E/ HOU SE/ AFTER/ SC HOOL.

I found Mila sitting with Lucy Hiller and Bigs Maloney. Lucy was eating today's hot-lunch special. It was spaghetti and meatballs. At least, they *looked* like meatballs. They probably *tasted* more like golf balls. How Lucy ate the stuff was a mystery to me. Yeesh.

Mila was singing. That was normal. You'd have to put a sock in her mouth to keep Mila from singing. Our teacher, Ms. Gleason, taught the song to us in class. It sounded like "On Top of Old Smokey," but the words were different.

Lucy and Bigs giggled while Mila sang.

"On top of spaghetti,
All covered with cheese,
I lost my poor meatball,
When somebody sneezed."

I said hi and handed Mila the note. She stuffed the paper into her pocket without looking at it. Then the bell rang.

Lunch was over.

But the case was just beginning.

Chapter Three

Room 201 Goes Batty

Back in room 201, Ms. Gleason told us, "This afternoon we're going to study a nocturnal animal." She looked around the classroom. "Would anyone like to tell us what *nocturnal* means?"

Bobby Solofsky yelled out, "It's an animal that sleeps all day and stays out all night!"

Ms. Gleason ignored him. She didn't like it when we called out answers — even when it was the right answer. She called on Danika Starling instead. "Thank you for raising your hand, Danika." As usual, Danika knew the right answer.

"Yesterday we talked about owls," Ms. Gleason said. "Today we're going to learn about bats."

"Yeah, I love baseball!" Ralphie Jordan joked.

Even Ms. Gleason had to laugh. Besides, it was hard to get mad at Ralphie Jordan — even when he didn't raise his hand. We talked about what we already knew about bats. Then we gathered in the reading circle. Ms. Gleason read a book called *Bats! Bats! and More Bats!* It had really cool pictures.

We broke into groups and made Venn diagrams, comparing bats to owls. They were a lot alike. Most bats and owls were predators. They hunted at night. We also listed the ways they were different. That was pretty easy, too. Owls are birds. They have feathers. Bats are mammals. They just *think* they're birds.

Later on, we made little brown bat stick puppets. It was fun. Except I sort of made a mess with the glue. I spilled some on the floor. Helen Zuckerman stepped in it. She was sort of upset.

Oh, well. Nobody's perfect.

Before cleanup, Ms. Gleason reminded us about the field trip on Monday. We were going to Four Rivers Nature Preserve. We were going to take a bus, and two parents were coming with us.

Everybody had to be prepared for rainy weather. Ms. Gleason said that we were going *rain or shine*. "Spring is right around the corner," Ms. Gleason said. "That means a lot of rain, because all those flowers and trees need water to grow."

Bigs Maloney said he hoped it would rain. That's Bigs for you. He's a stomping-in-puddles kind of guy.

"What will we do when we get there?" Joey Pignattano asked.

Everybody knew the answer. Even Joey. But it was like a good story. We wanted to hear it again.

"A guide will lead us on a hike around a beaver pond," Ms. Gleason reminded us. "We'll look at animal habitats. Where they live, what they eat. We'll *observe* and *draw conclusions*."

"How do you draw a conclusion?" I piped up. "With crayons?" Everybody laughed.

Except for Ms. Gleason. "Excuse me, Theodore Jones," she said. "I'm very tired of people talking while I'm talking." Ms. Gleason rubbed her eyes and her body sort of sagged. I guess she really was tired. Ms. Gleason took a deep breath. "We'll have a wonderful day. We'll have a picnic. And if the weather cooperates, we'll end the trip with a treasure hunt."

We couldn't wait. Sure, it wasn't Hoffberg's Playland, but a walk in the woods sure beat school.

"Okay, boys and girls," Ms. Gleason said. "It's been a long, hard week. Time for our Friday Cheer. Are you ready to scream your heads off?"

We sure were.

Ms. Gleason counted down, "Five . . . four . . . three . . . two . . . one!"

For ten seconds, we screamed our heads off. We hooted. We howled. We hollered and shouted. We shrieked. We screeched. We stomped, whomped, and roared. We yelled. We bellowed. And finally, we mellowed.

What a way to end the week!

Chapter Four

In the Tree House

When the weather was good, I used the tree house in my backyard as an office. Sure, maybe it wasn't the greatest place ever built. It was lopsided and it wobbled just enough to make you nervous. But it didn't matter to me. What mattered was . . . *it was mine*. See, the tree house was supposed to be for all the kids in my family — Billy, Hillary, Nicholas, Daniel, and me. But I've pretty much taken it over.

I climbed up and waited for Mila and Ralphie. I set out a pitcher of grape juice

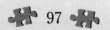 97

and three cups. I took a sip. Suddenly Mila's head popped up. "BOO!" she shouted.

Grape juice squirted out my nose. "Mila! You could have given me a heart attack. Yeesh!"

"Lighten up, Jigsaw," Mila said. "I was just practicing my sneak attacks. Pretty good, huh?"

I admitted that she was a good sneak. "But next time," I said, "practice on someone else."

Mila grinned.

"Hey," I asked, "why didn't Rags bark?"

"I gave him half a pretzel," Mila said. "That kept him quiet."

That was Rags for you. If you fed him once, he'd love you forever. I didn't mind. It was nice that Mila and Rags were becoming friends. See, Mila is allergic to fur. She had to stay far away from Rags. But Mila started taking a new allergy medicine. It worked. I was glad. All that sneezing can get on a guy's nerves.

I told Mila about my talk with Ralphie Jordan. She listened closely. Just then, Ralphie peddled into my backyard. He leaned his bicycle against the tree. Rags watched from his doghouse and barked twice. For Rags, that was his idea of making a big fuss.

Ralphie climbed the ladder. He fished a torn, crumpled dollar from his pocket. "Hold on to your money," I told him.

"I don't even know what you want me to do."

"I want you to make my problem go away," he said.

"What sort of problem?" Mila asked.

Ralphie glanced at Mila, then back at me. "She won't laugh?"

"Not unless you tickle her feet with a feather," I answered. I pulled out my detective journal. I wrote:

Friday, March 20th.
Client: Ralphie Jordan.

"Go ahead," Mila urged. "Nobody will laugh at you."

Ralphie took a long, slow sip of grape juice. "My house is haunted," he said.

Chapter Five

The Scream of the Crime

I poured myself another drink.

Ralphie continued, "When I go to bed, I hear weird noises."

"It's probably just the wind," Mila explained.

"Does the wind go *scritch-scratch* against the walls?" Ralphie asked. "Does the wind go *thump, thump, thump*? Does it rattle chains and moan in the middle of the night?"

"Maybe it's just a nighttime animal," I offered.

"Yes," Mila said. "It could be a nocturnal animal. Like an owl or a raccoon or . . ."

". . . or a moose!" I added.

"What?!" Mila asked.

I wiggled my fingers behind my head, like antlers. "You know," I explained. "A moose."

Mila shook her head and sighed. She faced Ralphie. "What did the moan sound like?"

Ralphie cupped his hands in front of his mouth. He started to moan — a long, low, spooky moan. "*WooOOoowoo. WOOoowooOOoo.*"

That was good enough for me. I opened my journal. I grabbed a marker and drew a picture of the suspect. It didn't exactly look like a ghost. Instead, I'd say it was a pretty good drawing of an upside-down sock . . . with eyes. Yeesh.

I looked at Ralphie, then nodded toward my glass jar. Ralphie poked the dollar into the jar.

"What now?" Ralphie asked.

"Now," Mila said, "we visit the scene of the crime."

We made it to Ralphie's in three minutes. His house, like spring, was just around the corner.

Ralphie lived in the biggest, oldest house on the block. It was two stories, with a high, sloping roof. Ralphie brought us onto the front porch. *Creak, creeeeak*. The chains of a bench swing groaned in the wind. "My mother's visiting cousins in Georgia," Ralphie said. "My father works at home. But I'm not allowed to bother him unless it's a real emergency."

He brought us upstairs into his bedroom. It was a large room with dark paneling on the walls. On one side the ceiling came

down in a sharp angle. It made the room feel cozy, like a cave.

"I see you like scary stories," Mila said, eyeing the bookshelves. She tilted her head and read some titles out loud. "*In a Dark, Dark Room. The Haunting of Grade Three. The Ghost in the Attic.*"

I looked out the window into Ralphie's backyard. There was a garden below. And beyond that, a lone willow tree on a green lawn. Off to the right, his brother, Justin,

was shooting hoops in the driveway. "Hey, Mila," I said. "I can see your house from here."

Mila came to the window. "You're right, Jigsaw. See that window? That's my room."

I turned away and prowled Ralphie's bedroom with my eyes. Everything seemed normal. "Well," I said. "I don't see any signs of a ghost."

"What did you expect?" Ralphie said. "Ghosts are nocturnal. They only walk the earth at night."

"Well, there's nothing else to do," Mila concluded. She folded her arms. "Jigsaw has to spend the night."

"I do?" I said. "But . . ."

"Great — a sleepover!" Ralphie yelled. "I'll go ask my dad."

Oh, brother. I always get the dirty work.

Chapter Six
The Sleepover

Saturday afternoon, I picked up the phone and dialed.

"Hello?" a voice answered.

"Is Ralphie there?"

"Excuse me?" the voice asked. It was Mr. Jordan.

I tried again. "Is Ralphie home . . . *please*?" All I heard was silence. Then I added, "This is Jigsaw."

"That's much better, Jigsaw," Mr. Jordan said. "Hold on. I'll get him for you."

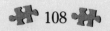

I told Ralphie it might be a good idea if Rags slept over, too. "He usually sleeps in my room," I said. "He'd be scared without me."

Ralphie was thrilled. He asked his father. Mr. Jordan said it was fine with him. I knew it would be. Ralphie's dad was a dog person. When we were on vacation in Florida, the Jordans watched Rags for a whole week. And they didn't even hate it.

I took a bath and even used soap. My hair was washed and combed. My socks were matched. My underwear was clean. I was everything a detective should be. Until I tried on my new secondhand pants.

"Mom!" I yelled down the stairs. "I am NOT wearing Nick's old jeans."

My mom climbed the stairs, muttering. "What are you talking about?" she said. "You look fine." She rolled up the pant legs. "There, that's better!"

"Mom, they're too baggy. I can't go to Ralphie's like this. I look like Shaggy on *Scooby-Doo*."

"Those jeans are perfectly fine."

"But . . ."

"No buts, Theodore," she said.

"But . . ."

Then she gave me . . . the look.

It meant: *End of discussion*.

Oh, brother.

I threw my things into a backpack. Toothbrush, pajamas, detective journal,

extra markers, a water bowl and a bone for Rags. Then I went downstairs and grabbed the house flashlight. I didn't ask permission. It was too big a risk. My mom might have said no.

Ralphie and his brother, Justin, were playing catch on his front lawn. Justin Jordan was fifteen years old. He was tall and strong and he could run like the wind. He loved sports. Any sport. Sometimes Justin teased us, but he was usually pretty nice . . . for a teenager.

Justin bent down and gave Rags a playful push. "Hey, Ragsy. Remember me?" he asked. Rags answered by wagging his tail. He remembered.

"Rags is sleeping over, too," Ralphie told Justin. "He's going to be our watchdog."

"Watchdog?" said Justin. "What for?"

Ralphie looked around. He whispered, "You know. What I told you about. *The ghost.*"

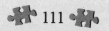

111

Justin laughed out loud. "Ghost!" he said. "Don't be ridiculous. Ghosts aren't real. It's just your imagination."

Ralphie wasn't buying a word of it. "Go ahead, don't believe me," he said. "See if I care. But you'll be sorry when he sneaks into *your* room and scares *you* to death."

Chapter Seven
The Ghost Story

Mila joined us at Ralphie's house for pizza dinner. Later we played Frisbee football in the backyard. The teams were Justin and Mila against me and Ralphie. I'd like to say we won. But I can't. Because we lost.

Mostly, though, we waited for the ghost to come. We watched as the sun fell from the sky. Long shadows filled the backyard. The wind started to blow. Leaves danced in the trees. And like a woolly blanket, darkness wrapped around us.

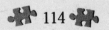

Mr. Jordan came out onto the porch. "Okay, kids," he said. "It's getting late and it looks like a storm is kicking up. Better come inside."

Before Mila left, we went over the plan one more time. We were going to use flashlights to signal each other from the windows. Three short flashes meant we were okay. Two long flashes meant . . . trouble.

"What do I do if it's two long flashes?" Mila asked.

"Call the ghostbusters," Ralphie joked.

Nobody laughed. "You'll think of something," I told her.

Suddenly the sky burst with rain. It poured. It rained cats. It rained dogs. It rained hippos and elephants, too. The rain got so bad, Mr. Jordan had to give Mila a ride home — even though she only lived around the corner.

Mr. Jordan let us stay up to watch a

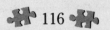

video called *Zombies Ate New Jersey*. He even made popcorn for us. There wasn't much else to do after that but go into Ralphie's room and wait for the ghost. We laid our sleeping bags on the floor. Rags curled up in the corner of the room.

"I'm not very sleepy," I said. "Are you?"

Ralphie sat up with a smile. "No way, José!"

There was a knock on the door. "You guys still awake?" It was Justin. He came

into the room carrying a box. "Any sign of that ghost?" he asked.

"Not yet," Ralphie said.

Justin sat cross-legged on the floor. He placed the box in front of him. "Well, I hate to spoil your little sleepover, but there's no such thing as a ghost." Justin paused. Then he leaned forward and said, "But if you want, I *could* tell you a spooky story."

I looked at Ralphie. He nodded. Yes.

Justin looked around the room and

frowned. "Not dark enough," he said. He turned off one light, then another. I could barely see his face.

"Wait a minute," Ralphie said. He turned on my flashlight and pointed it away from us. Eerie shapes perched on the wall, like a row of black crows.

"Once upon a time . . ." Justin began. He spoke softly, in a whisper. We leaned forward to hear. ". . . on this very spot. Long, long ago. A man was killed."

I felt Ralphie grab my wrist.

"I know this is true," Justin said. "Because I found this box when I was digging near the old willow tree." He put his hand on the box. "But I'm sure you don't want me to open it. Do you?"

Ralphie nodded again. Yes. He did.

Nobody asked me.

Justin reached over and turned off the flashlight.

Suddenly it was as dark as a mummy's tomb.

Justin opened the box. . . .

Chapter Eight

Eyeballs in the Dark

It was too dark to see. I listened closely and felt Ralphie's body pressed close to mine.

"In this box," Justin said, "is the rotting flesh of the man's dead body."

"For real?" I asked.

"*Shhhh*," Ralphie hushed.

Nah, I thought. It can't be for real. It's just a story.

"Put out your hands," Justin said. He placed two round, slippery balls into

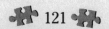

my fingers. They felt like marbles, but squishier.

"Those were his eyes."

Yeesh. I handed the eyeballs to Ralphie.

Justin gave me something else. It was small and soft and a little bumpy. It bent in my fingers.

"That was his ear."

My stomach felt funny. I handed the ear to Ralphie.

"This is the worst, most disgusting, most

horrible part," Justin whispered. "You're not scared, are you?"

We didn't answer. I don't even know if we breathed.

"Here. I've put it on the floor," Justin whispered. "Feel for it." Ralphie's hands and mine fumbled in the dark. I felt something slimy. In the darkness, I tried to figure out the shape. It had long, curved pieces, like fat worms. I counted them.

One, two, three, four . . .

Justin said, "It was . . ."

". . . his HAND!" I shouted.

"Aaaaaaarrrggghhh!" Ralphie screamed. He jumped up and flicked on the lights.

Justin fell back on the floor, laughing.

With the lights on, we could see the body parts.

The "eyes" were two peeled grapes.

The "ear" was a dried apricot.

The "hand" was a rubber glove filled with mud.

Still laughing, Justin picked himself up off the floor and strolled to the door. "Chill out, guys. That's the only scare you're gonna get tonight. There's no such thing as a ghost."

I was glad to see Justin leave.

Maybe now I'd stop trembling.

Suddenly I remembered. "Mila!" We rushed to the window. It was still raining, but not as hard as before. We signaled three times. Nothing happened. We did it again. We searched through the darkness. Nothing.

"Look!" Ralphie finally cried. There it was, three flashes in the window. It was Mila.

Once again, we got into our sleeping bags and turned off the lights. "Hey, Jigsaw," Ralphie said. "Want to hear a joke?"

"Sure."

"What do ghosts eat for dessert?" he asked.

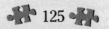

"I dunno," I answered.

"Ice scream!" Even in the dark, I could make out Ralphie's bright white smile. Then he yawned.

A minute passed. "You sleepy, Ralphie?" I asked. "Ralphie?"

He was out like a light.

Oh, brother. I lay awake in a dark, dark room, thinking that this was one of Mila's worst ideas ever. And I tried to fall asleep. I mean, I *really* tried. But all I could think of was ghosts . . . and eyeballs . . . and creepy noises.

Scritch-scratch.

Nah, just the wind, I told myself.

Scritch. Scritch. Scraaaatch.

The noise seemed to come from the wall nearest me. I tried to forget about it by humming a happy tune. *Hum-de-dum, de-dum-dum.*

Then it started. Just as Ralphie had described it.

WooOOoowooOOoowooOOoo.

I lifted my head and looked around the room. Soon there were more sounds. *Thump. Thump. Thump.* I looked up. In the corner of the room, I saw two yellow eyes.

They were floating in the dark.

Scritch-scratch. Thump, thump, thump. WooOO-wooOOoo.

The eyes were coming closer.

And closer.

Right then, I knew for sure:

I was a goner.

Chapter Nine
The Night Visitor

SLURP!

A giant tongue licked my face.

"Ragsy, old pal!" I said. The floating eyes were his! My big, friendly, drooling, ever-loving dog! I was never so happy to get licked in all my life.

My happiness quickly vanished when I heard a scream. It came from downstairs. Then nothing. Just dead silence.

Don't ask me why. But I *had* to see what it was. I grabbed my flashlight. Ralphie was still sleeping. "Come on, Rags," I whispered.

My big, brave dog clip-clopped across the floor. At that moment, I was glad Rags wasn't a French poodle. I crept down the darkened stairway. *Thump, thump, thump.* I stopped to listen. Whew. It was only the pounding of my heart. Then I heard another shout. A muffled voice cried, "Get him! Get him!"

I jumped when a hand suddenly grabbed my shoulder. . . .

"Jigsaw, what's up?"

I turned. It was Ralphie.

I put a finger to my lips. "I think it's somewhere down there."

"What's down there?" Ralphie asked. He was still half asleep.

"The ghost," I whispered.

"NO! NO!" begged the voice.

Ralphie smiled. "Oh, that's just my

father," he said. "He's probably watching a basketball game. He always shouts at the players."

Just then, Rags bolted down the stairs, through the living room, and into the den. Mr. Jordan, holding a bowl of pretzels, came out to the bottom of the stairs. He squinted into the flashlight. "Ralph? Jigsaw? Turn that flashlight off, will you? What are you doing up at this hour?" Rags stood by his side, hoping for a pretzel.

Ralphie stammered, "Um . . ."

"Rags needs water," I said.

Mr. Jordan gave us a funny look. He gave Rags a pretzel. "Okay, boys. Then right back into bed. No more funny stuff."

We went into the kitchen. I gave Rags some water. He lapped it up. Then I searched the cupboards. I found what I needed above the sink. It was a box of Rice Krispies. "Can we take this upstairs?" I asked Ralphie.

"I guess so," he said. "Why?"

"You'll see," I answered.

Back in Ralphie's room, I gave Rags a bone to keep him busy. Then I poured the cereal on the floor. "This is a ghost alarm," I said. "If the ghost comes into the room when we're sleeping . . ."

". . . we'll hear *snap, crackle, pop!*" Ralphie said.

For the third time that night, we crawled back into our sleeping bags. We kept all the lights on. I must have fallen asleep, because I woke to a noise. It was a step.

Then another. Then another. Louder and louder. Closer and closer.

I woke Ralphie. "Something's coming," I whispered.

The doorknob slowly, slowly turned. *Eeeek*. The door opened.

After that, a lot of stuff happened at once. Things got pretty mixed-up. Ralphie pulled the sleeping bag over his head and started screaming, "Don't eat me! Don't eat me! Don't eat me!"

Rags started running around the room in circles, barking like crazy.

I looked up and saw Mr. Jordan at the door. He looked pretty scared himself. He came into the room — *crunch, crunch, snap, crackle, pop, crunch* — and started waving his arms around.

I hollered at the top of my lungs, "RAGS, BE QUIET!"

After a while, Ralphie stopped screaming.

Rags stopped barking.

And Mr. Jordan just stood there with his hands on his hips. He looked at Ralphie. He looked at me. He looked at Rags. He looked at the Rice Krispies on the floor. Then his head swung back to Ralphie, then back to me. Mr. Jordan didn't move for a long, long time. He sighed. He ran his strong fingers over his mustache. He sighed again.

"Is everyone calm?" he finally asked.

We nodded. Rags wagged.

"Ralph, Jigsaw," Mr. Jordan slowly said. "I want you to come with me. And boys," he added, before leading us down the hall, "you had best clean up this mess in the morning."

Finally, at long last, we fell asleep. All of us. Me, Ralphie, and Rags. Huddled together. Snug as bugs in a rug.

In Mr. Jordan's very crowded — and very safe — king-size bed.

Chapter Ten

Nature Detectives

I woke up early on Sunday. Mr. Jordan made waffles while Ralphie and I cleaned Ralphie's room. Sweeping up all those Rice Krispies made us hungry. After breakfast, I went home. I needed a nap.

On Monday, we headed to Four Rivers Nature Preserve for our field trip. It felt good to get away from ghosts for a while.

Mila sat on the bus next to me. "I think I saw something the other night," she told me. "In Ralphie's backyard."

"What do you mean . . . *saw something*?" I asked.

Mila leaned close to me. "I kept trying to signal you with my flashlight. But you didn't answer, except for that one time." She paused. "I saw a shape moving around."

"What kind of shape?" I asked.

Mila shook her head. "I couldn't tell. It was too dark. But it might have been a person."

"Or a ghost," I added.

The bus came to a stop.

I was surprised when I saw our guide. I expected somebody with a big ranger hat. But this guy had a magnifying glass and a hat like Sherlock Holmes! His name was Hal Roberts. He brought us into the Nature Center. It was a small museum. In the back room, there was a large window overlooking a field. We all took turns with the binoculars, looking at the birds in the feeders. The best part, though, was Aristotle. He was in a glass cage set into the wall. Mr. Roberts told us that Aristotle was a white-barred owl.

He told us a sad story. A couple of years ago, a nice lady found Aristotle on the side of the road. The owl had been hit by a car and was badly injured. She took Aristotle to an animal doctor. The doctor saved Aristotle's life. But Aristotle lost a wing in the accident. He would never fly again.

Now he lived at Four Rivers, stuck inside a cage for the rest of his life. I felt bad for Aristotle. Ralphie and I tried to cheer him up with a few hoots.

Aristotle didn't give a hoot back. I guess I didn't blame him.

Then we started our hike. It was called the Beaver Pond Trail. After a little while, Mr. Roberts made us stop and look at something. It was a pile of brown pellets. In other words, deer poop!

Mr. Roberts told us we were lucky. "With all that rain this weekend, the ground is nice and muddy. Perfect for animal tracks." He asked us to become nature detectives. We had to look around for signs of animal life. He called them clues.

"I think I found something!" Mila shouted.

"Good detective work," Mr. Roberts said. "This is an animal track." Mr. Roberts pointed out the hoofprints. He said it was a deer track. He poured plaster of paris into the track. "When the plaster hardens, it will form a mold. Then you can take it back to your classroom."

"For keeps?" Geetha asked.

"For keeps," Mr. Roberts answered.

It was a great day. Mr. Roberts taught us to look closely at things. He pointed to a row of holes on a tree. We had to guess what kind of animal made the holes. Helen Zuckerman guessed that it was a woodpecker. She was right.

After the hike, we had a big picnic. Ms. Gleason let us run around and act wild. Then we had a scavenger hunt. We had to use our skills as nature detectives to find all sorts of things. I found something that told us the wind was blowing. That was easy — the leaves on the trees. Mila found empty acorns. We drew the conclusion that they had been eaten by something. Probably a squirrel. Ralphie even discovered a

bird's nest. But we weren't allowed to touch it.

In the end, we learned that nature tells us stories. But nature doesn't use words. Nature tells us in its own language.

It really was like being a detective. If you looked at things closely enough, the clues would tell you a story.

Chapter Eleven

The Mysterious Footprints

We decided to play nature detective as soon as we got home from the field trip. Ralphie's yard was the biggest, so that's where we went. But first I stopped home to get my magnifying glass. We looked for animal clues. I guess Ralphie found the first clue. He stepped in dog poop.

I patted Ralphie on the back. "Nice work, Detective."

While Ralphie changed into sneakers, Mila and I searched the garden for animal tracks. Mila found a centipede. I let it crawl

on my hand. Only it didn't crawl much. After a while, we decided it was probably dead. Yeesh.

"Hey, Jigsaw," Mila said. "Look at this." She was behind the bushes, next to the house. Mila picked up a broom. "What's this doing here?" she asked.

I held up my magnifying glass. The broom was caked with clumps of dry mud. Looking down, I suddenly shouted, "Footprints!" Ralphie joined us as we gathered around the mysterious footprints.

"Any conclusions?" I asked.

Ralphie shrugged. "I guess somebody walked back here."

"But why?" I said. "There's nothing here."

We thought it over for a while.

"What about that strange shape you saw the other night?" I asked Mila.

"Yes," she said. "It was right around this area."

Suddenly I understood everything. The broom . . . Mila's mysterious shape . . . the large footprint. The clues were coming together.

And they were telling a ghost story.

I gazed up at the side of the house. Up high, near Ralphie's window, I saw tiny streaks of mud. "Let me try something," I said. I held the broom high and rubbed it against the wall. We listened closely.

Scritch. Scratch.

I banged the broom against the wall.

Thump. Thump. Thump.

"I understand now," Ralphie said. "The ghost used this broom to make the scary sounds."

Mila knelt beside the footprints and stared through the magnifying glass. "I don't think so," she said. "Unless you know any ghosts who wear Nikes."

We sent Ralphie inside. He came back in a minute . . . holding a pair of Justin's sneakers. "It was easy," Ralphie explained. "Justin left them in the mudroom."

As I suspected, the sneakers were Nikes. And they were muddy and damp. I turned a sneaker upside down and held it next to the footprint. "A perfect match," I said.

I put my hand on Ralphie's shoulder. "You don't have a ghost," I told him. "You have something far worse." I paused. "You have a *teenager.*"

Ralphie asked, "But how did Justin make the *woo-woo* noises?"

"I'm not positive," I answered. "Probably the same way you did, back at the tree house." I cupped my hands over my mouth. "*WooOOoowooOOoowooOOoo.*"

The three of us marched into Ralphie's house. Justin was eating a bowl of cereal in the kitchen. I held the broom in my hands. Mila held the sneakers. And Ralphie pointed at his brother. "You're the ghost!"

Chapter Twelve

Justin Gets All Wet

Justin confessed everything.

"But why?" Ralphie asked. "You scared me to death."

Justin smiled. "Admit it," he said. "You loved it."

And I guess Justin was right. It was fun thinking there was a ghost on the loose. Sort of.

Of course, we still had to get him back. Fair is fair. And I knew just how to do it, too. It was an old prank my father showed me. About half an hour later, we found

Justin in his bedroom. He was lying on the floor with his head between the stereo speakers.

"Want us to show you a trick?" Ralphie asked.

Justin said, "Nah, too busy."

"Come on," Ralphie urged. "You owe me."

Justin groaned and stood up. I stepped forward, holding a small bucket of water. I said, "I can make this bucket stick like magic to the ceiling. Want to see?"

I climbed up on Justin's desk. I mumbled some fancy mumbo jumbo. Stretching on my toes, I held the bucket of water against the ceiling. "It takes a minute to stick," I explained. After a little while, I told Justin that my arm was getting tired. "You're the strongest," I said. "Could you please hold this for a while?"

Justin groaned. "Better yet," I said. "Just grab that hockey stick. You can stand underneath it and hold it from there."

Justin grabbed the stick. I did my best not to smile. He pressed it firmly against the bucket. I climbed down. Mila and Ralphie giggled. Then we said, "Thanks a lot, Justin. See you later!"

We ran out the door, leaving Justin in the room standing under a bucket of water. "Hey, guys! When are you coming back?" he yelled. "Hey, get back here! What do I do with the bucket?!"

We ran into the backyard, laughing our

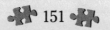

heads off. In a few minutes, Justin came out to find us. His shirt looked wet. But he was smiling. "Nice trick, you guys," he said. "I suppose I deserved it."

Just then, Mr. Jordan pulled into the driveway. Justin looked at his father. He looked back at us.

There was a twinkle in his eye.

Justin walked toward the car. "Hey, Dad," Justin called out. "Want to see how I can make a bucket of water stick to the ceiling?"

Ralphie turned to me and smiled. It was a Ralphie Jordan Special.

Well, that's it, I thought. For a dollar a day, I make ghosts go away. Another mystery solved. It was like a puzzle with all the pieces in place. Nothing to do now but rip it up and start on another one. I knew there would be more cases. More mysteries to solve. And I'd be waiting — ready to piece the clues together.

That's why they call me Jigsaw.

The Case of the
Stolen Baseball Cards

Dedicated to the memory
of Raymond Chandler,
for the creation of the
greatest gumshoe
of them all,
Philip Marlowe

Contents

Chapter One

Eddie's Baseball Cards

I got up. I got out of bed. I dragged a comb across my head.

Wednesday morning — oh, brother. It was as exciting as a bowl of oatmeal.

Here's the thing. I was a detective without a case. That's like being a hamburger without a bun. It's like being Mike Piazza without a pitch to hit. I needed a mystery to solve. I mean, what good is a detective if he isn't fighting crime?

I sat at the breakfast table, drinking grape juice and waiting for the toaster to

pop. The sky was as blue as a swimming pool. A voice on the radio was talking about Indian summer. I checked the backyard. No Apaches in sight.

"It's not fair," my eleven-year-old brother, Nicholas, moaned. "Kids shouldn't have to go to school on nice days like today."

"Yeah," my oldest brother, Billy, agreed. "We should all take the day off and drive up to the lake. What do you say, Dad?"

My father looked up from his newspaper and frowned. "I wish we could," he said. "But we can't. So stop complaining and eat your breakfast."

That was my dad for you. He was an ogre in the morning. In the Jones family, we've learned to give Dad plenty of room until he drinks his coffee. But after that — *abracadabra* — he turns into a pretty great dad. That coffee sure works wonders.

After polishing off my second plate of frozen miniwaffles, I hurried to the bus

stop. Mila skipped out of her house when I arrived. She was lucky — the bus stopped in front of her house.

As usual, Mila was singing:

"Oh, take me out to the ball game,
Take me out to the crowd.
Buy me some peanuts and pizza,
I don't care if we never get back."

"Pizza?" I asked. "Don't you mean Cracker Jacks?"

"I like pizza better," Mila explained. "Cracker Jacks get trapped in my teeth."

Mila and I are in Ms. Gleason's class together — room 201. But we aren't just classmates. We are partners. We solve mysteries together.

For a dollar a day, we make problems go away.

When the bus pulled up, I suddenly realized I had my own problem to solve. I forgot my lunch box. That meant buying hot lunch in the school cafeteria. Oh, brother, mystery meatballs again.

Yeesh.

There was a crowd of kids already on the bus. Mila and I walked to the back and sat down. Eddie Becker had a blue binder open on his lap. Everybody was leaning over their seats to see it.

Eddie bragged, "Smart baseball card

collectors, like me and my uncle Max, collect rookie cards."

"Wow, you've got Sammy Sosa!" Mike Radcliffe exclaimed. "Slammin' Sammy is my favorite!"

Kim Lewis, her wild hair flying out from underneath a Yankees cap, squealed when she saw Derek Jeter's rookie card. "He's *sooooo* awesome!"

Mila said to me, "That Eddie's got a great collection. I bet it's worth a lot of money."

"Big whoop-de-do," I mumbled.

I'll be honest. I wasn't exactly president of the Eddie Becker Fan Club. I thought he was a show-off. And you didn't need to be a detective to see it. The proof was right there at the back of the bus.

Chapter Two

Stolen!

All the kids in room 201 acted like Eddie's baseball card collection was the greatest thing since Nintendo.

Trust me. It wasn't.

I was so not interested. I had to tackle the Lunch Problem. I walked up to Ms. Gleason's desk and tried to look as sad as possible. "I forgot my lunch," I moaned. "I might not make it."

Ms. Gleason chuckled to herself. "You remind me of my basset hound. He makes the same face when he wants something.

Don't worry. Before lunch you can take a buddy to the secretary's office. Mrs. Vega will give you a dollar from petty cash."

That was a relief. Sure, I might be poisoned from eating mystery meatballs. But at least I wouldn't starve to death.

Suddenly I heard Eddie's voice get loud and angry. "Hey, don't grab!" he told Bobby Solofsky. "That card's in mint condition."

"Mint condition?" Bobby said. "It's got jelly stains on it!"

Ms. Gleason interrupted, "Look with your eyes, boys and girls. Remember our classroom rules." She pointed to a poster on the wall. She read rule number nine, *"Respect other people's things."*

The bell rang. We stood for the Pledge of Allegiance. When we were all seated, Eddie walked over to the closet. He looked at Ms. Gleason, shrugged, and explained, "I forgot something." Eddie hung his backpack on a hook and slid his blue binder onto the top shelf.

Eddie Becker had blond hair and blue eyes — and he was crazy about baseball. Eddie wore the same baseball shirt every single day. He knew every statistic for all the players. Eddie Becker was a walking, talking baseball encyclopedia. But I think he loved his baseball cards most of all.

When Eddie returned to his seat, Ms. Gleason announced, "Today we're going to start a new project called 'All About Me.'"

She reached down behind her desk and lifted up a suitcase.

"All right, field trip!" Ralphie Jordan piped up. "We're going to Disney World!"

Everybody laughed, even Ms. Gleason. "I thought it would be nice if we could get to know one another a little better," Ms. Gleason said. "First I'll share some things about me." One by one, Ms. Gleason took things out of her suitcase. She showed us her running sneakers, ski goggles, a jar of seashells, and a few photographs. There was even one of her in a basketball uniform!

"Wow," Athena Lorenzo said. "Did you play in the WNBA, Ms. Gleason?"

Ms. Gleason laughed. "No, the WNBA wasn't around when I played," she said. "But I did play college ball."

Ms. Gleason told us about Brutus, her basset hound. Those are the goofy-looking dogs with short legs and long ears. "He's a

piece of work," Ms. Gleason said. "Brutus will eat anything — even my smelly socks!" Everybody laughed. I liked that Ms. Gleason had a dog. My dad says there are two kinds of people in the world: dog people and cat people. He says that I'm a dog person. I was glad to learn that Ms. Gleason was a dog person, too.

Ms. Gleason pulled out a banner made out of construction paper and tacked it to the wall. The banner had her name on it and lots of crayon pictures. The pictures, she told us, were of her favorite hobbies.

"Tonight for homework," Ms. Gleason said, "I'd like you to make your own banners." She even gave us our own blank banners to fill in at home.

When the rest of the class lined up for lunch, I went with Ralphie Jordan to the secretary's office. Then we went to meet our class in the cafeteria.

After lunch we played outside for a

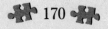

while. Ms. Gleason usually reads to us after recess, so we plopped down on the carpet in the reading circle. Playing was hard work and we were all a little tired.

While we waited for story time, Eddie got up to check on his collection. He pulled down the binder, opened it, and exclaimed: "My cards! They're gone!"

He held up the binder for everyone to see.

The pages were empty!

Chapter Three

The Phantom Leaves a Clue

Eddie looked around the room. "Somebody stole my baseball cards!"

No one said a word. We just sat there, shocked.

"Who did it?" Eddie demanded. "Was it you, Bigs?" Eddie pointed an accusing finger at Bigs Maloney. "Or was it you, Kim? You're the one who made such a fuss over my Derek Jeter card."

Ms. Gleason spoke up. "That's enough, Eddie," she said in a stern voice. "No one is pointing fingers in my classroom."

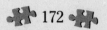

"But —"

"No buts," Ms. Gleason said, her face turning red. "I know you're upset. But please return to your seat. I'll handle this."

Mila raised her hand. "Excuse me, Ms. Gleason!" she said.

"What is it, Mila?"

Mila stood up. "When Eddie picked up the binder, I noticed that a scrap of paper fell to the ground. Maybe it's a clue."

Eddie rushed over to pick up the paper. He read it, then held up the note for everyone to see. It read:

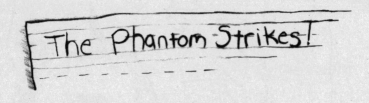

The Phantom Strikes!

Everybody started talking at once, until Ms. Gleason made us settle down. Ms. Gleason was unhappy, and she didn't try

to hide it. The kids were worried and upset.

After all, there was a thief in room 201.

I took out my detective journal. I couldn't find my red marker. So I picked up my next favorite color. I wrote in green:

The Case of the Stolen Baseball Cards.

Below that, I made two neat columns. At the top of one, I wrote Suspects. On the other, I wrote Clues.

I turned to a new page and wrote:

Who is the Phantom????

Meanwhile, Ms. Gleason went over to Eddie and talked to him quietly. Then she stood up in front of the class. "Boys and girls, this is serious. Eddie says he had twenty-six baseball cards in his binder."

"He did," Helen Zuckerman chimed in. "We all saw them."

Ms. Gleason nodded. "Okay," she said. "The cards are missing, and I'm very, very upset. We all know never to touch someone's personal property. But maybe someone took the cards by accident. Please look in your desks."

No one found a thing. Except Joey Pignattano. He found an old Oreo stuffed in the back of his desk. Joey twisted it open,

licked the white insides, and gobbled down the cookie part in two bites.

I scribbled a message to Mila in secret code. It was pretty easy to read, once you knew the trick. You had to cross out every other letter. That's why detectives call it an Alternate Letter Code.

I handed the page to Mila. It looked like this:

MQEWERTY MUEP ASTA TFHJEL
OMFBFCIZCTEI ALFKTHEDRR SXCVHZOKOPL.

Here's what it really said:

MQEWERTY MUEP ASTA TFHJEL
OMFBFCIZCTEI ALFKTHEDRR SXCVHZOKOPL.

Chapter Four

A Bargain

After reading the note, Mila slid a finger across her nose. That was our secret signal. In the detective business, you can't be too careful. That's why we use codes and secret signals. I looked around the room. Bigs Maloney, Joey Pignattano, Lucy Hiller, even my pal Ralphie Jordan — anyone might be the Phantom.

Out on the playground for afternoon recess, everybody was talking about the robbery. Most kids felt bad for Eddie. But Kim Lewis was mad. She said Eddie was wrong to accuse her. I agreed with Kim. You

can't accuse someone until you have proof. Solving a mystery is like doing a jigsaw puzzle. It's not solved until all the pieces are in place.

I wanted to talk to Eddie Becker — *alone*. But I had to wait for him to finish talking with Bigs Maloney. I couldn't hear what they were saying, but Bigs looked pretty unhappy. I guessed that Bigs didn't like being accused, either. Believe me, you don't want to mess with Bigs Maloney. We didn't call him "Bigs" for nothing.

I finally grabbed Eddie and handed him my business card. Actually, it was an index card with Mila's neat handwriting on it:

Need a Mystery Solved?
Call Jigsaw Jones
or Mila Yeh,
Private Eyes!
For a Dollar a Day,
We Make Problems Go Away!!!

Eddie looked at the card and yawned. He handed it back to me. "No thanks," he said.

"Don't you want your baseball cards found?" I asked.

Eddie stared at me for a minute. Then he smiled. "Tell you what," he said. "If you want to try to solve this case, that's fine with me. But I won't pay you."

"Sorry, Eddie," I said. "It doesn't work that way."

Eddie scratched at the ground with his sneaker. "I'll make a deal with you" he said. "If you solve the mystery, you can have any one of my baseball cards. But if you don't solve it by tomorrow," he said, "you have to pay me a dollar."

"Tomorrow," I said. "That's rough."

"Well, if you can't do it . . ."

"*Any* card?" I asked.

"You can take your pick," Eddie answered.

"It's a deal." We sealed it with a handshake.

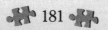 181

"Let me see the Phantom's note," I said. Eddie handed over the paper. I studied it under my magnifying glass. I slipped the note into my pocket. "I'll keep this," I said. "It's evidence."

Eddie shrugged. He didn't seem to care one way or the other.

Finally it was the end of the school day. Everybody had jobs to do in room 201. We all had to clean up our area and sharpen our pencils. Plus, some kids got special jobs. There were Homework Checkers and Closet Neateners, Board Cleaners and Eraser Stampers and chair Putter-Uppers.

Mila was the Homework Checker that day. Me and Ralphie were Chair Putter-Uppers. Danika Starling was Zookeeper. We had two hamsters in our class, Romeo and Juliet, and they needed food and fresh water every day. We all agreed: Zookeeper was the best job in the classroom.

When we lined up to leave, Ms. Gleason said, "Before you go, boys and girls, I want everybody to empty their backpacks. It's a good time to clean out old papers."

Ms. Gleason didn't fool me for a minute. I knew that she was still hoping to find Eddie's missing baseball cards. We all dumped out our packs. But there were no cards to be found.

"I'm sorry, Eddie," Ms. Gleason said. "They don't seem to be anywhere."

I wasn't surprised.

The Phantom wasn't going to be caught that easily.

Chapter Five

In the Tree House

Mila met me at my tree house after school. I could hear her coming from a mile away. She sang:

"Root, root, root for the home team,
If they don't win, it's a bummer.
'Cause it's one, two, three strikes you're out
At the old ball game!"

Mila climbed up the tree house ladder. I handed her my magnifying glass and the note. "The paper's torn," I said. "And look."

I pointed to the red and blue lines on the page. "It's the same kind of paper we use for homework."

Mila studied the note. "Red marker," she murmured. Mila rocked back and forth, thinking. "The writing is all squiggly and wiggly," she said.

"Yeah, like it was written by a first-grader," I said.

Mila ran her fingers through her long black hair. "Or maybe," she said, "the

Phantom did it on purpose."

"Could be," I said. "Handwriting is like a fingerprint. The Phantom probably wrote it extra sloppy as a disguise. Too bad," I sighed. "I guess this isn't much of a clue."

That's when Mila turned the paper over. "Hey, Jigsaw," she said. "Look at this."

There were some letters, written neatly in pencil, on the back.

"Yeah," I said. "So?"

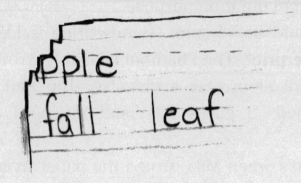

pple

fall   leaf

"Jigsaw, don't you remember?" Mila said. "These are some of the words from last night's vocabulary homework."

"*pple?*" I asked. "What's a *pple*?"

"The page is torn," Mila said. "The front letter is missing."

I thought for a minute. Then I thought for another. I was on my third minute of Deep Thinking when Mila blurted out, *"Apple!"*

"I was just about to say that," I complained.

"There's something else," Mila said. "I recognize this handwriting. This page came from Kim's homework!"

 188

Chapter Six
Kim's Story

I opened my detective journal. "Now we're getting somewhere. Boy, I'm good at this detective stuff." I poked Mila in the ribs. "Just kidding, Mila. Nice work."

Mila looked down, embarrassed.

Under the word **Suspects**, I wrote the name **Kim Lewis**. I circled it in orange. "Kim's our best suspect," I said. "Eddie also accused Bigs Maloney." I wrote down his name, too.

"It could be anybody," Mila said. "Even you."

"Me?" I said.

Mila smiled. "Well, it is written in marker — and everyone knows you always carry around a set of markers. Plus," she added, "when the whole class went to the cafeteria, you were walking the hallways. You could have stolen it then."

"You don't really think . . ."

"Nah." Mila laughed. "I can be a kidder, too, you know."

For a joke, I added my name to the list of suspects. Then I said in a deep voice, "Jigsaw Jones, did you do it?" I answered myself, "Nope. I'm innocent."

I crossed out my name. "He says he didn't do it," I told Mila.

She just shook her head.

I slugged down the last of my grape juice. "We need more facts," I concluded. "Let's go have a little talk with Kim Lewis."

Kim lived three blocks away. On the way

over, Mila and I discussed the case. I told her about my deal with Eddie.

"Hmmm," Mila said.

"What do you mean *hmmm*?" I asked.

"Nothing," Mila answered, "Just *hmmm*."

I stopped. "Well? Is it a good *hmmm* . . . or a bad *hmmm*?!"

Mila lifted her shoulders and let them drop. "It's just a *hmmm-hmmm*."

Oh, brother. We walked on. "I saw Bigs Maloney and Eddie talking on the

playground," I said. "Bigs didn't look too happy."

"Bigs scares me," Mila said. "He's so . . ."

". . . big," I said, finishing her sentence. I didn't tell Mila that Bigs scared me, too. Because he didn't. I knew the big lug was basically a nice guy. He just . . . sort of . . . made me a little . . . *nervous*.

Kim was playing catch with Nicole Rodriguez. They were practicing their grounders and pop-ups. They were pretty good.

"Hey, guys, want to play?" Kim shouted.

"Can't," I said. "We're on a case."

Kim threw a high pop to Nicole.

I showed Kim the note — but only the side with her handwriting on it. "Recognize this?" I asked.

Across the yard, Nicole made a nice running catch.

"Time-out!" Kim yelled. She looked closely at the note. "Hey, that's from my

homework. Where'd you get this?"

I turned the note over. Kim read the words: THE PHANTOM STRIKES!

Kim looked at us, confused. "I don't understand," she said.

I got right to the point. "Are you the Phantom?"

"No," Kim said, smiling. "I'm the Easter Bunny!" She jutted out her front teeth and hopped across the yard.

Yeesh. I was surrounded by loonies.

Mila interrupted, "Kim, I was the Homework Checker today. You didn't hand in your homework."

Kim stopped hopping. "Do you think I stole Eddie's cards?" she said. "Nice friends. Thanks a lot — and see ya later."

Kim started walking away. "Come on, Nicole. We're out of here."

Mila called after her, "Don't get mad, Kim. We didn't mean . . ."

Kim spun around. "Listen, I did my

homework last night. I brought it to school. Then I lost it. End of story."

"Lost it?" Mila asked. "When?"

Kim made a face. "If I knew that, I wouldn't have lost it." She went inside the house with Nicole. The door slammed shut.

"Do you believe her?" Mila asked.

"I don't know," I answered. "Maybe, maybe not."

Mila closed her eyes, lifted her chin, and let the sun's warm rays wash over her face. She frowned. "I've got to get home," she said. "We've done enough damage for today."

"Go ahead," I said. "I'm going to catch up with Bigs Maloney."

"Good luck, Jigsaw," Mila said.

"Yeah," I answered. "I'll need it."

Chapter Seven

A Pain in the Neck

Mrs. Maloney answered the door. She held one baby in her arms. Another baby was on the ground, grabbing her leg. "You've met the twins, haven't you?" she asked. "This is Harry. And the little guy sucking on my knee is Larry."

That's the thing with twins. They all look alike. To make things worse, Harry and Larry dressed alike. "How do you tell who's who?" I asked.

"Oh, a mother knows," Mrs. Maloney

said. "But here's a tip: Larry has a big freckle on his nose. Harry doesn't."

"Is Bigs home?" I asked.

"Yes, he's in the family room. He's supposed to be doing his homework." She wiped Harry's nose with a tissue. "But I think he's watching television."

I found Bigs in the family room. There was no homework in sight. But that wasn't the weird thing. Bigs was dressed in red long johns and a red long-sleeved shirt. He

wore blue underwear on top of his long johns. Bigs wore a mask over his face. And a black cape.

The letter *P* was taped to his chest.

Bigs was jumping up and down on the couch, throwing fake punches. He was watching a wrestling match on TV.

"Jigsaw, you gotta see this," Bigs urged. "The Red Phantom is about to pin the Terrorizer!"

I didn't have much choice. You don't

argue with Bigs Maloney. After the match, Bigs clicked off the TV. "Let's wrestle," he said. "I'll be the Red Phantom. You can be the Terrorizer."

"Er, but Bigs," I stammered. "Wrestling isn't really my —"

Wham! Before I knew it, Bigs pounced on me. Then he twisted my body into the shape of a pretzel.

"Pinned!" Bigs shouted, thrusting his fists into the air. "The Red Phantom triumphs again!"

He looked down at me. "You all right, Jigsaw?" he asked.

I tried to wiggle my fingers. They still worked. "Is there a doctor in the house?" I said.

Bigs laughed. "You're funny."

"Yeah, funny," I groaned.

Bigs helped me up. "I'm going to be a professional wrestler when I grow up," he told me. "Either that . . . or a florist."

"A florist?"

Bigs laid his huge paw on my shoulder. He had the grip of a grizzly bear. "Yeah, what's the matter? You don't like flowers?"

I told Bigs I liked flowers. I *loved* flowers. Some of my best friends were flowers. Finally he released his grip. My shoulder ached. But at least it was still attached to the rest of my body.

"Want to wrestle again?" Bigs asked. "I need to practice my double knee drop."

"Uh, er, I'd love to, really," I said, backing

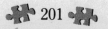 201

up. "But I'm in a hurry. I came to ask you a few questions about Eddie Becker."

"Don't even say that guy's name," Bigs said. "He owes me a baseball card. Now Eddie says he can't pay me back."

As Bigs told it, I wasn't the only guy he mangled in a wrestling match. Last week, Bigs and Eddie watched wrestling on TV together. Then Bigs pinned him — six times in a row.

"We made a bet," Bigs said. "If I won, I was allowed to take my pick of his best baseball cards."

I thought it over. "But without any cards," I said, "he can't pay you."

"Almost," Bigs said. "Eddie's still got plenty of cards. But they're all *commons*. I wanted one of his prized rookie cards."

"What's a *common*?" I asked.

"Every year they print thousands of baseball cards," Bigs explained. "Some of them will be worth a lot of money

someday. But most cards," he said, shaking his head, "will never be worth anything. They're called *commons*. Most collectors don't want 'em."

I scribbled notes in my journal. Then I got out of there in a hurry. I didn't know what a double knee drop was — and I sure didn't want to find out.

It sounded painful.

Chapter Eight

Grams

I limped home, aching and tired. This detective business was hard work. My big, clumsy, ever-loving dog jumped up and licked my face. "Rags, no! Stop it! YUCK!"

One minute I was a pretzel. The next, I was a human Popsicle. Oh, brother. I could start my own restaurant.

My mom called to me from the kitchen. "Dinner should be ready soon, Theodore," she said. "Why don't you get cracking on that school project of yours?"

That's my mom for you. Somehow she

always knew about my homework — even when I forgot all about it. I went into my room and pulled out the banner that Ms. Gleason gave us. I wrote my name across the top: **JIGSAW JONES**. I used different colors for each letter. I thought about my favorite hobbies.

I drew a picture of a big magnifying glass. Inside I wrote **Finding Clues**. I drew pieces of a jigsaw puzzle. I wrote **Puzzles**. Then I drew a self-portrait. I wrote **Drawing**.

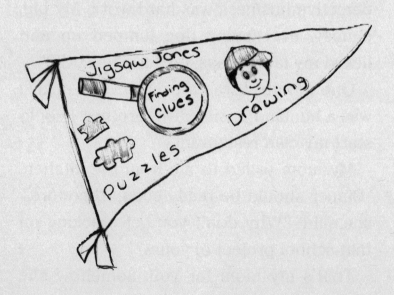

There was a knock on my door. "Dinnertime, Shorty!" That was my sister, Hillary. She's thirteen.

I didn't exactly love being called "Shorty."

But I guess it beats "Peanut."

Grams had everyone laughing at dinner. Grams is my mom's mom. She lives with us now, because after Grandpa died she didn't like being alone. That was fine with me. I love Grams. And besides, she always gives me butterscotch.

Grams told us about the first time my dad picked up Mom for a date. "I didn't like him!" she said, laughing at the memory. "He had a big, bushy beard. He wore dirty jeans with patches all over them. And he had a long ponytail!"

Hillary laughed so hard, she squirted milk through her nose. That made us laugh even more.

"Hey, hey," my dad said. "It was the seventies. Everybody dressed like that."

"I know, dear," Grams said, patting his hand. "You can't judge a man by his clothes. But I'm glad you don't dress like a hippie anymore."

After dinner I asked my mom if she knew anything about baseball cards. "Don't ask me," she said. "Grams is the baseball expert in this house."

"Grams?" I said.

My mom just smiled. "Go ask her," she said.

 208

Well, people will surprise you. Just because you see the outside of someone, it doesn't tell you what's *inside*. I guess Grams learned that about my dad. And I was learning it about her.

Grams brought me into her room. She pulled out an old tin from her night table. Inside, wrapped in a rubber band, were some old baseball cards. I mean, *really old* baseball cards.

"Are these worth a lot of money?" I asked her.

Grams waved her hand. "Who knows?" she said. "Probably not. These cards are like me, old and worn-out. Collectors like to keep them in plastic, shiny and new. But I'd never sell them. These cards help me remember the old days."

She touched the tip of my nose with her finger. "When you get to be my age, memories are worth more than money."

We sat and talked for a long time.

Actually, Grams talked. I just listened to her scratchy voice. She told me stories about the old days. About going to Fenway Park with my grandfather to see Ted Williams and the Boston Red Sox. "He was some ballplayer," Grams recalled. "I always loved the Red Sox . . . and I still do."

She got quiet for a while, just picturing it in her mind. The green grass, the noisy crowd, and my grandfather in his wide straw hat. Then she whispered, almost to herself, "Those were happy, happy times."

That's the last thing I remember.

I fell asleep in her lap.

Chapter Nine

Figuring It Out

I woke up in a panic. I dreamed I was being chased by a slobbering, hairy giant. I felt its hot breath on my neck. I felt its claws dig into my back. . . .

I was squished against the wall. My blanket was gone. I rolled over to find Rags hogging the bed. His paws pushed into my back. To make things worse, he was drooling on my pillow.

"Oh, Rags." I sighed. "Give me a break." I tried to push him off. The big fur ball wouldn't budge. Yeesh.

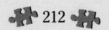 212

I wondered if cat people had days like this.

I suddenly realized: Today was the day. If I didn't solve the case, I'd owe Eddie Becker a dollar. Time was running out.

I washed and ate breakfast in a hurry.

Briiing, briiing. The phone rang.

"Who could be calling this early?" my mom wondered. She answered the phone, then handed it to me.

"Jigsaw, this is Mila. Can you come right over after breakfast?"

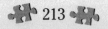

Two minutes later, I was leaning on her doorbell.

Mila and I sat down on her front steps. "A few things about this case have been bothering me," Mila said.

I flicked a pebble with my thumb and listened.

"Eddie didn't seem sad enough," Mila said. "If I lost something that I loved, I'd want to cry."

"Maybe Eddie's not the crying type," I said.

"Maybe," Mila said. "But the thing that really bothers me is how Eddie discovered the robbery."

"What do you mean?" I asked. "He wanted to check on his cards. That's normal."

"I guess," Mila said doubtfully. "But why did he look *inside* the binder? If it was me, I would have checked to see if the binder

was still there. I wouldn't have thought to open it."

Mila had a point. Why did Eddie look inside? Unless . . . Eddie already knew the cards were gone.

I told Mila that Eddie owed Bigs Maloney a baseball card.

Mila smiled. "You found the missing piece, Jigsaw! Eddie had a *motive*."

"A motive?" I asked.

"Yes, a *reason* for faking the robbery! With his best cards stolen," Mila explained, "Eddie wouldn't lose one to Bigs."

It was starting to make sense. "But what about the search?" I asked. "We all had to empty our backpacks."

"*All* of us?" Mila asked. "I don't remember Ms. Gleason looking in *Eddie's* backpack. After all, no one suspected that Eddie stole his own baseball cards."

The bus pulled up.

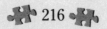

"I guess Eddie's the Phantom," I concluded. "But we've still got one problem."

"What's that?" Mila asked.

"How did Eddie do it?"

Chapter Ten

The Confession

I sat by the window, watching the world roll past. Eddie was in his usual spot, joking with Bobby Solofsky and Mike Radcliffe. He wore the same identical baseball shirt. Only today I noticed something different. It had an old ink stain on the shoulder.

I thought about Bigs Maloney's twin brothers, Harry and Larry. I thought about Grams — and how the outside of something didn't always tell what was inside.

And I suddenly knew how Eddie Becker pulled off the crime.

The bus dropped us off at school. We still had a few minutes before class. "Hey, Jigsaw," Eddie called out. "You owe me a dollar." He held out his palm. "Pay up."

A few kids gathered around — Mila, Bobby, Bigs, and Kim Lewis.

I didn't reach into my pocket. "You seem

pretty happy for a guy who lost his best baseball cards," I said.

Eddie let that one pass. "Pay up," he repeated.

I turned to Bigs. "Hey, Bigs," I said. "You ever notice how Eddie always wears the same shirt? Tell me — what kind of guy would wear the same old smelly shirt day after day?"

Eddie shifted on his feet.

"Doesn't your mother ever wash that thing?" I asked him.

"You don't know anything," Eddie said. "I have two of the exact same shirts. When one is in the wash, I wear the clean one."

It was just as I thought. "Except one shirt has an ink stain on the shoulder, right?"

Eddie looked at the stain. "So?"

"So," I said. "You've got two shirts that look alike. No big deal. Bigs has two brothers who look alike. It happens. Except I figure you've got two blue binders that look alike. Don't you, Eddie?"

Eddie's face turned pale.

"Yesterday you brought two blue binders to school, didn't you?" I asked. I held up two fingers. "Not one binder, Eddie. Two."

Eddie turned to leave. "You're crazy."

A large hand with the grip of a grizzly fell on Eddie's shoulder. "Not so fast," Bigs Maloney said.

"Yeah, Eddie," Kim Lewis said. "Not so fast."

Eddie looked at our faces, scared and silent. He was caught, and he knew it.

"One binder had cards," I said. "You made sure to show them to everybody. Then you made the switch. I figure you had an empty blue binder in your backpack. It was a nice trick, Eddie. Especially when you put away the empty binder in the closet for everyone to see. Real smooth.

And the phony note," I said, "that was a nice touch. You had me fooled for a while."

"Is that true, Eddie?" Bigs asked.

Eddie nodded and hung his head. "I'm sorry," he said. "I'm really sorry. It's just . . . well . . . I love those cards so much."

Chapter Eleven
The Phantom Strikes . . . Again!

Mila gave me a high five. "Jigsaw, that was awesome!"

"Thanks," I mumbled.

Even Kim Lewis patted me on the back. "Nice work, detective!" Kim wasn't mad at us anymore.

Ms. Gleason and Eddie talked quietly in the hallway for a long time. None of us could hear a word. And believe me, we tried. When they came back, Eddie looked almost happy — and Ms. Gleason was back to her smiling self.

 225

"Okay, boys and girls," Ms. Gleason said, clapping her hands. "I can't wait to see those banners!"

By the end of the day, room 201 looked like my backyard on laundry day. Our banners dangled from two long ropes stretched across the classroom. They were hung with clothespins. We loved it. Now room 201, Ms. Gleason said, was "All About Us."

After school, I bicycled with Bigs Maloney to Eddie Becker's house. It was payback time. Walking into Eddie's room was like entering the Baseball Hall of Fame. There was a big poster of Mark McGwire, plus hundreds of baseball pictures cut out from magazines. Eddie had baseball bedsheets, baseball trophies, baseball books — even a baseball garbage can.

Eddie had hundreds of cards filed neatly in storage boxes. Those were his commons, the ones that weren't worth much. He kept his best cards in plastic "card guards," stored in three-ring binders.

I didn't waste time. I told Eddie exactly what I wanted. He was thrilled. Eddie happily gave me four quarters and my pick from his commons.

I chose one. "It's not worth anything," Eddie pointed out. "He's just a backup catcher, and the card's not in great shape."

I looked at the card. On the bottom it

read "Boston Red Sox." I slid it into my pocket. "Maybe not to a collector," I said. "But it will be worth something to a friend of mine."

Bigs, meanwhile, picked out Eddie's most prized treasure. A Ken Griffey Jr. rookie card. Poor Eddie looked like someone had just drowned his cat.

Bigs studied the card, reading all the facts and stats. He looked at poor, miserable Eddie Becker. "I can't take this from you," Bigs said.

"Wh . . . wha . . . what?" Eddie said.

"I can't take it," Bigs said. "You love it too much." He handed the card back to Eddie, who stood there amazed.

"But you still owe me one thing," Bigs said. He jabbed a thick finger at Eddie's chest.

"Sure," Eddie said. "Anything."

Bigs winked at me. "Good," he told Eddie. "Let's wrestle!"

Then Bigs pounced — wham!

I left the room to the sound of Eddie's moans and groans. I heard Bigs Maloney scream, "Pinned! The Red Phantom triumphs again! Get up, Eddie." Bigs urged, "Let's wrestle again!"

I was happy to wrap up another case. I hopped on my bike. First I had to drop off fifty cents at Mila's house. She deserved it. Without her help, I would have never

solved the case. Then I had to find Grams. I had a present for her. It was just a common baseball card, but I knew it would make her smile.

And that was worth more to me than money.

The Case of the
Mummy Mystery

To my editor, Helen Perelman
— for loving Jigsaw from the beginning,
for believing in mummies,
for putting up with me,
and for correcting my mi[s]takes.
(Not that I ever make any.)

Yeesh!
-HP

CONTENTS

Chapter One

Guess He'll Go Eat Worms

I'm a detective, and I solve mysteries.

Some cases are nice and easy. Somebody loses a cat. I find the cat. They pay me, and everybody's as happy as a bug in a rug.

Then there are the tough cases. The cases that wiggle and turn like a worm on a hook. The mysteries that are full of surprises.

This was one of those cases.

I *thought* it was going to be a simple job. But one thing's for sure. I never expected mummy trouble.

 237

That's right. I said mummy. Not mommy. *Mummy*.

Mommies I can handle. *Mummies* are a different story. A mummy is a walking zombie. He's a guy covered with bandages who looks like he jumped off a tall building without a parachute. He's a guy who was dead and buried — but then came back to walk the earth.

That kind of mummy.

Yeesh.

It all started with a dare. At least that's the way Joey Pignattano told it. We were in my office, a tree house in my backyard. As usual, Joey Pignattano's mouth was moving. But I couldn't believe what my ears were hearing.

I glanced at my best friend and partner, Mila Yeh. Her arms were folded across her stomach. Her face looked pale, like she was going to be sick. As Joey talked, Mila's eyes

blinked open and closed, open and closed, like the flashing lights of a Christmas tree.

Mila couldn't believe what Joey was saying, either.

I interrupted Joey, speaking slowly and carefully. "Hold on, Joey. Let me make sure I've got all the facts." I read from my detective journal. "You are telling us that you are going to eat . . . a worm."

Joey's head bobbed up and down enthusiastically. "For a dollar," he added, smiling proudly.

"For a dollar," I repeated. "Well, that's not something you see every day." I scratched the back of my neck. "Are you going to eat it plain? Or with ketchup?"

Joey's eyes got wide. "Great idea!" he exclaimed. "I never thought of ketchup!"

"It's something to think about," I told him.

Mila shot me a look. I ignored her and

continued. "Are you going to swallow the worm whole? Or chew on it?"

Joey bit his lip. "Dunno," he said. "Depends on the worm."

Mila looked at us like we were both nuts. But I had to admit. I sort of liked the idea of Joey Pignattano eating a worm. Like I said before, it's not something you see every day.

"Wait a minute," Mila said. "Who is paying you the dollar?"

"Bobby Solofsky," Joey answered.

"When are you eating the worm?" she asked.

"Friday," Joey said.

"That's Halloween," I said.

Joey nodded. It sure was.

Mila just shook her head. "Don't you think that eating a worm is sort of . . . gross?"

Joey shrugged happily. He didn't particularly think so.

"So why do you need a detective?" I said.

Joey leaned close. "I don't want to get cheated," he whispered. "I don't trust Bobby — he's trouble."

I wouldn't trust Bobby Solofsky, either. But then again, I wouldn't eat a worm for a dollar. I guess there are two kinds of people in the world. Some eat worms. The others, well, they just don't.

Picky eaters, I guess.

"I could make sure you don't get

cheated," I assured him. "But I make a dollar a day. Can you afford me?"

Joey stared hard into my eyes. "Would I eat a worm if I had that kind of money?" he asked.

I saw his point. Joey Pignattano was flat broke. "OK, Joey," I said. "You can owe me."

So that's how this whole mess started.

The mummy didn't come into it until later on.

Chapter Two

Not Hungry

That night before dinner, my brothers Daniel and Nicholas were messing around in the playroom while I did my spelling homework. I had to write each word five times and put them in ABC order.

Black	Halloween
Candy	~~Pumpkin~~
Children	October
Frightened	Pumpkin
Ghost	Spooky
~~Frightened~~	Treat

While I worked, I listened to my brothers talk. "Every Halloween," Daniel said to Nicholas, "he prowls through town, causing trouble everywhere he goes."

I looked up from my homework. "Who does?" I asked.

"And he eats stray cats," Daniel said.

"Who does?" I asked again.

"And he loves mischief," Daniel said.

"GUYS!" I yelled. "WHO loves mischief?"

"Don't tell him," Nicholas said. "He'll have bad dreams."

"Tell me WHAT?" I demanded.

"Nothing," Daniel answered.

"Please," I pleaded. "What are you guys talking about?"

Daniel sighed. "OK. But you have to promise not to tell Mom and Dad."

"I promise," I said.

"Do you promise on a stack of Batman comic books?" Nicholas asked.

"I promise," I repeated. "Now tell me: *What are you guys talking about?!*"

Daniel looked around cautiously. "Not here," he said. "Down in the basement."

Suddenly, my mother called out, "Dinner's almost ready. Theodore, it's your turn to set the table."

"MOM!" I complained. "Please don't call me Theodore. Everybody calls me Jigsaw."

My dad came into the room. In a funny voice he said, "I don't care WHAT you call me . . . as long as you call me for dinner."

Then he gave my mom a big, sloppy kiss. Oh, brother.

Daniel gave me a poke. "After dinner," he whispered. "In the basement."

I smiled. Secrets are almost as much fun as mysteries.

My mom set out a big, steaming bowl of spaghetti and meat sauce. "Joey Pignattano is going to eat a worm for a dollar," I announced.

"That's very nice, dear," my mother said. "Please pass the spaghetti, Billy."

I continued, "I wouldn't eat a worm, no matter how much you paid me."

"I'm proud of you, son," my father mumbled.

I stared down at my plate of spaghetti. "I think Joey is crazy. Worms are so slippery and slimy and gross." I put down my knife and fork. "Sort of like, er, spaghetti."

"Jigsaw!" my sister, Hillary, protested. "Gross me out the door!" She spit out something into her napkin.

"Hey, hey," my father said. "No talk of worms at the dinner table."

One by one, my brothers pushed their plates away.

"What's wrong?" my mom asked.

Billy frowned at me. "Sorry, Mom," he said. "I just don't feel hungry anymore."

"Me, neither," Daniel and Nicholas said.

Hillary complained, "All this talk about eating worms has spoiled my appetite — *especially* for spaghetti."

Grams didn't seem to pay any attention. She just kept shoveling huge forkfuls into her mouth. Grams finally winked and said, "Eat up, kids. These worms are delicious."

Chapter Three
The Legend of the Mummy

An hour later, I followed Daniel and Nicholas down into the basement. My oldest brother, Billy, was already down there. He was rebuilding an old car engine. His face was marked with black grease. A million different parts were laid out on newspaper.

Billy looked up from unscrewing some kind of whatcha-ma-call-it. "What's up?"

"We're going to tell Jigsaw about the Halloween legend," Daniel explained. "You know — the mummy."

 250

Billy nodded slowly, staring hard at Daniel. "Oh, yeah," he said. "The mummy. Don't you think it might scare him too much? I mean, he's only a pip-squeak."

"Am not," I protested.

Daniel sighed. "OK, OK. You know what a mummy is, right?"

"Sure," I joked. "He's like Frankenstein's cousin. Or nephew, or something."

They laughed at me.

"Hey, I'm kidding," I said. "A mummy is a movie monster. He was in one of my puzzles, 'The Monsters of Hollywood.'"

Daniel shook his head. "Yeah, but this one is real, and he lives right here in town."

"Yeah," Billy said. "The mummy rises from his wormy grave and comes alive every Halloween."

Billy got up, arms outstretched, and walked stiffly across the room. He moaned and groaned. He tried to grab me by the throat. But I ducked out of the way.

"Remember Mrs. Estep's cat, Twinkles?"
Daniel asked.

I remembered.

"Remember how it disappeared two
years ago at Halloween?"

I still remembered.

"The mummy got it," Billy said.

"How do you know?" I asked.

"Barney Fodstock saw it happen," Daniel
said.

Billy went on, "And you know Mr. Reilly, the old guy with white hair who lives on Charlie's Hill? His hair used to be jet-black."

"So?"

"So his hair turned completely white in one night," Billy said. "Because he saw the mummy and nearly died of fright."

A chill ran down my spine. Which was weird, because I didn't really — *really, really* — believe in mummies.

But still, it was hard to know for sure.

Chapter Four

It's a Mystery

When I got to the bus stop the next morning, I found Joey Pignattano staring into his hand.

"What are you doing, Joey?" I asked.

"Training," he answered.

I looked closer. An ant crawled on Joey's palm.

Joey closed his eyes, brought his hand to his mouth, and swallowed. The poor ant never knew what hit him. One minute he was crawling around, searching for a

crumb. The next minute the little guy was trapped inside Joey Pignattano's belly.

What a way to go.

Joey licked his lips and shrugged. "Not so bad," he said.

"Sure," I said. "Better than Raisinets. But a tiny ant is not exactly a squishy worm."

"I know," Joey said earnestly. "I'm working my way up the animal kingdom."

Yeesh.

Mila skipped out of her house. The minute she saw Joey, Mila started singing:

> *"Nobody likes me,*
> *Everybody hates me,*
> *Guess I'll go eat worms.*
> *First you peel the skin off,*
> *Then you chew the guts up,*
> *Ooey-gooey wooorms!"*

When the bus pulled away, I watched as Mila's house got smaller and smaller until it was the size of a bug. "Did you decide yet what you're going to be for Halloween?" Mila asked me.

I shrugged. "I don't know. A pirate, I guess. Or maybe a gorilla. Or Frankenstein, I think, maybe. How about you?" I asked.

Mila smiled. "Here's a hint. *I vant to suck your blood!"*

We both laughed. Mila was going to be a vampire. "My stepmom, Alice, is sewing me

 257

this really cool black cape. And I already have a set of plastic fangs."

Then I told her what my brothers had told me. About the mummy . . . and how he walks through town on Halloween . . . and causes all sorts of trouble.

Ralphie Jordan, who was sitting in front of us, turned around. "It's true," he said. "Barney Fodstock even saw the mummy with his own eyes."

"How do YOU know?" I asked.

"Everybody knows about the mummy," Ralphie said. "It knocked down Earl Bartholemew last year."

Earl Bartholemew was an eighth-grader who lived across the street from Ralphie. "Are you sure?"

Ralphie's eyes lit up, bright and large. "It was Halloween night. Earl was in a hurry, so he cut through Greenlawn Cemetery. Suddenly, he felt someone push him in the back. Earl fell and chipped a tooth. But

when he turned around . . . no one was there."

"Maybe he tripped," I said.

Ralphie shook his head. "No, Jigsaw. He was *pushed*."

"Well," Mila said, pulling on her long black hair, "it sounds like a mystery to me."

I pulled out my detective journal. I turned to a new page. With an orange marker, I wrote: **THE CASE OF THE MUMMY MYSTERY**. "This looks like a job for Jigsaw Jones, Private Eye."

Chapter Five

Halloween Fever

Halloween was nearly here. Everybody in room 201 was ready to explode with excitement. Our teacher, Ms. Gleason, said she was going to send the whole class to the nurse. "You kids have a bad case of Halloween Fever."

We sure did. We were really looking forward to the Halloween parade. All the parents were going to come. Even Grams. And it was the same day that Joey Pignattano was going to eat a worm. What more could you ask for?

Meanwhile, the story of the Halloween mummy swept through the class like a hurricane. The more kids talked about it, the better the stories got. Now even Bobby Solofsky claimed that he had seen the mummy. I didn't know about that. But one thing was sure: We were all going to stay far away from Greenlawn Cemetery.

Ms. Gleason was excited, too. But she wasn't thinking about mummies. "I really want to win the teachers' pumpkin pie contest this year," she told us. "Ever since last year's disaster, I've been working extra hard in the kitchen."

"What happened last year?" Danika Starling asked.

Ms. Gleason buried her face in her hands. "I left my pie on the radiator at school on the day of the contest. By the time the judge saw it, my beautiful pie was melting. You could have eaten it with a straw!"

Then Ms. Gleason cheered up. "But this

is my year," she said. "I'm going to make the most beautiful, most delicious pumpkin pie this school has ever seen — and I'm *not* going to leave it on the radiator!"

"I don't like pumpkin pie," complained Athena Lorenzo. She squinched up her face. "It tastes too . . . *pumpkiny*."

Ms. Gleason walked to the blackboard. "Well, OK, then. Everyone break into groups. We've got a lot of work to do."

Ms. Gleason was the best teacher in

the school. She made learning fun. This week's theme was Halloween. All week long, every activity had something to do with Halloween. So we didn't even mind learning.

On Monday, Ms. Gleason draped a white sheet over the big stuffed chair for story hour. She drew two black eyes on the sheet. We all took turns sitting in the ghost's lap for story hour. Even better, we read spooky stories every day.

On Tuesday, we played Halloween Bingo with our vocabulary words. We did Spider Math on Wednesday. Every group got a spider s body with a different number on it. My group Mila, Joey, Geetha Nair, and me got number seventeen. Then we had to pick out the legs that added up to seventeen and attach them to the body. I attached 9 + 8 and 19 - 2. Joey Pignattano tried to attach 1 + 7, but Mila wouldn t let him. In art, we made really cool bat mobiles.

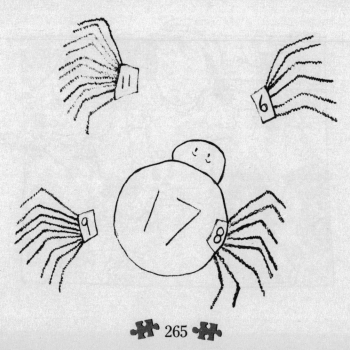

Meanwhile, I did a little work on Joey's case. First I caught up with Bobby Solofsky in the cafeteria. He was sitting with Bigs Maloney, Lucy Hiller, and Eddie Becker. "Joey told me about your dare," I said.

Bobby slid his tongue across his teeth and made a sucking noise. "Yeah, so what," he said.

"I'm supposed to make sure everything's fair and square," I told him. "Joey doesn't want to get cheated."

"Cheated?! *By me?!*" Bobby placed his hand on his chest. "I'd never cheat anyone."

"Sure, Solofsky," I said. "You're a regular Boy Scout. But just in case, why don't you let me hold onto the money. This way it won't get lost."

Bobby shook his head. "Aw, Theodore," he said — Bobby called me Theodore just to bug me — "you can trust me."

"Sure I can," I replied. "But I don't. I'll be watching you, Solofsky. You better not try any funny business."

Chapter Six

Eddie's Big Idea

Eddie Becker pulled me aside after lunch. "Hey, Jigsaw," he said. "Is Joey really going to eat a worm for a dollar?"

I shrugged. "You know Joey. What do *you* think?"

Eddie smiled. "I think he's crazy enough to do it."

I nodded. Joey was *definitely* crazy enough to do it.

"But you're going about this the wrong way," Eddie said. "He could make a lot more than a dollar if you let me help."

 268

"How?" I asked.

"Sell tickets," Eddie said. "I bet you a lot of kids would pay a quarter to watch him do it."

I thought it over. "Well, it's not something you see every day."

Eddie offered to be in charge of selling tickets. "But I want pay for my work," he said. "I get half. Joey gets half."

It was a deal. We shook hands right there. Now Joey would be able to pay the dollar he owed me.

"One more thing," I added. "Tell Bobby that *I'll* bring the worm."

Back in room 201, I found a note inside my desk. It was in code:

> blue the witch candy purple mummy
> and tall man green is like door monster
> red going brown to trick treat orange
> get black you!

I knew the note was from Mila. She liked to test my brainpower. This one was called a color code. The only words that really mattered were the ones that came right after color words. So I circled all the color words. Then I underlined the words that were next in line.

I looked up and saw Mila smiling at me.

I grabbed my throat and made a choking sound. Then my head fell on the desk, as if I had suddenly dropped dead.

At recess, Ms. Gleason gave Mila and me permission to visit the school library. We wanted to learn more about mummies. We found a good book called *Mummies! Mummies! and More Mummies!*

I was a good reader. But Mila was a fantastic reader. It didn't matter how many words were in the book or how squished together the words were. Mila could read just about anything.

I looked over her shoulder while Mila flipped through the pages. She'd read a little bit, say, "Hmmm," or "Boring," or "Yuck," and flip the page. When she said "Yuck," I always made her read it out loud.

Here's the thing. Long ago in Egypt, they used to make mummies all the time. That's because the Egyptians didn't want the bodies to get all juicy. The Egyptians believed they would need their bodies later on in a place called "The Afterlife." The Afterlife was their idea of heaven.

It took seventy days to make a mummy. The grossest part was when they scooped

out the brain. They did this by sticking a long spoon up the dead guy's nose!

Yeesh.

Then the embalmer — the guy who was in charge of making mummies — took out the dead guy's stomach and guts and stuff. Then they dried the body out with a special salt called natron and wrapped it up nice and tight like a birthday present.

Presto! One mummy, coming up!

Ding! The bell rang. We had to get back to room 201.

Oh, well. At least now I understood why mummies were so grumpy. They've all got headaches!

Chapter Seven

Worms in a Box

Mila came over after school. It was the day before Halloween and we had a lot to do. I went into my garage and got a shovel. "What's that for?" Mila asked.

"Worms," I said.

We went into the backyard and dug for worms. My dog, Rags, watched us closely. I think he was hoping for a bone. I turned over a rock. "Wow, look at all of them!" I exclaimed.

I asked Mila, "Which one looks the yummiest?"

Mila rolled her eyes.

"Joey should choose," I decided. "I'll give him a nice selection. Mila, we need a box or something."

Mila ran inside my house and came back with a square box about three inches tall. "Your dad gave it to me," she said.

I scooped the worms into the box. I tossed in some dirt and rocks, just so they'd feel at home.

That night, I got my costume together and shoved it into my book bag. I put the box of worms into a 3rd Street Food Market bag and went to bed. After I flicked off the light, my door nudged open. *Clomp, clomp, clomp.* Rags climbed into bed with me. I held him tight and fell asleep, dreaming of candy and costumes, worms and mummies.

The next morning it was Halloween. *Finally.* I saw Joey Pignattano at the bus stop. He seemed quiet, nervous. "Are you ready, Joey?"

He nodded solemnly. "I think so," he said.

I patted my grocery bag. "I've got a nice selection of worms for you, Joey. Fat ones, skinny ones, you name it."

Joey stared into the bag. "Can they breathe in there?" he asked.

"Don't worry," I said. "The worms are just fine."

On the bus, Ralphie turned around in his seat and smiled at Mila and me. "I learned a

new poem yesterday." He beamed. "Want to hear it?"

"Not really," I said.

Mila shushed me. "Go ahead, Ralphie."

"My brother, Justin, taught it to me. It's pretty gross," he warned.

"We can take it," Mila said.

"You're supposed to say it when you pass a cemetery," he explained. He looked out the window. There were no graves in sight. "But this is a special occasion."

Ralphie cleared his throat.

"The worms go in, the worms go out.
They crawl in your stomach
And out through your mouth.
Your teeth decay, your body turns gray,
And that's the end of a wonderful day."

The poem was a big hit. Pretty soon, everyone on the bus was repeating it. I

guess you could say we were just a bunch of poetry lovers.

Our plan for Joey was set. He was going to eat the worm during afternoon recess. Eddie Becker said he'd already sold eleven tickets. I took out my journal and figured out the math. Eleven quarters added up to two dollars and seventy-five cents. Now Joey could pay me with Bobby's dollar and still have money left over. Everything seemed perfect.

Then disaster struck.

Chapter Eight

The Robbery!

It never could have happened on a normal school day. But Halloween was anything but normal. "Total chaos," Ms. Gleason called it. And I guess she was right. It wasn't a big day for learning.

"What did you boys and girls have for breakfast this morning?" she asked. "Flubber? You're practically bouncing off the walls."

We all laughed. Ms. Gleason was pretty funny sometimes.

A lot of the kids brought in their

costumes. Some didn't. That's because their parents would pick them up for lunch. They'd go home, eat lunch, and get dressed. Then everyone would hurry back to school for the one o'clock Halloween parade.

I hung my book bag on a hook. Because my cubby was so crowded with junk, I placed my worm bag on the closet floor. Parents started arriving at around eleven o'clock. Everyone complimented Ms. Gleason on her costume. She was dressed up as a basset hound, complete with long ears and white-tipped tail.

I got dressed in the school bathroom right after lunch. It wasn't easy. Fortunately, the janitor, Good Old Mr. Copabianco, helped me draw stitches on my neck and forehead.

"Finished," he finally announced.

I stepped before the mirror.

"Needs blood," I observed.

 281

Mr. Copabianco rubbed his chin thoughtfully. "I've got just the thing," he said, and rushed out the door. He came back whistling. Mr. Copabianco had a can of red paint and a brush in his hand.

He added a few dabs of paint. "Nice and gruesome, Mr. Jones," he said admiringly. Good Old Mr. Copabianco!

I still had plenty of time before the parade. I was glad, because I wanted to check on the worms. Maybe Joey was right. Maybe they did need air.

I went to the closet.

I looked low. I looked high.

But my bag was gone.

Who in the world would steal a box of worms?

Chapter Nine

An Eyewitness

I told Mila that the worms were missing.

We immediately walked over to Bobby Solofsky. "Is this another one of your tricks?" I asked.

Bobby was dressed like a football player. "No tricks, Frankenstein," he replied. "I'm a quarterback. I don't pull bunnies out of my hat. Besides, I don't know what in the world you're talking about."

I watched him closely. Bobby looked me right in the eye when he spoke — and he never blinked. He was telling the truth for a change. Go figure.

"Ms. Gleason, did you see anyone take my bag?"

"No, Theodore, I didn't," she answered. "Today has been so hectic with people coming and going. What kind of bag was it?"

I told her it was a brown bag with red handles.

"Was it from the 3rd Street Food Market?" she asked.

"Yes," I said hopefully.

"I know exactly what it looks like," she said. "I used the same kind of bag for my pie today. I'll keep my eye out for it."

Ms. Gleason greeted Nicole Rodriguez and her mother. Nicole was dressed as a giant grapefruit. Suddenly, Bigs Maloney, dressed like a professional wrestler, entered the room. "Ms. Gleason, I'm back," he announced.

"You found it OK?" Ms. Gleason asked him.

"Easy as pie," Bigs said, smiling widely.

"Jigsaw," Mila said. "If someone took that bag, then there must be witnesses. Let's ask around. Maybe somebody saw the thief."

Mila had better luck than me. She was back in five minutes. "I found a witness," Mila said.

Mila stood beside Helen Zuckerman, who was dressed like Wonder Woman.

I pulled out my journal. "What did you see, Helen?"

"This may sound crazy," she said, "but I saw someone walking down the hall carrying a bag."

"What kind of bag?" I asked.

"Um, brown, with red handles, I think."

"Did you get a good look at who had the bag?" I asked.

Helen glanced at Mila. "Tell him," Mila urged.

"Well, um, sort of."

"Sort of?" I said. "What do you mean, *sort of*?"

Helen looked me in the eye. "I saw him. But at the same time, I didn't see him."

I closed my journal. "Helen, you may be a witness to a crime. Tell me exactly what you saw."

"He was . . . he was a . . . mummy."

"A mummy!" I exclaimed. "Surely you're kidding."

"Don't call me *Shirley*," Helen said.

"Huh?"

"My name is Helen. Don't call me Shirley."

"I DIDN'T call you Shirley," I explained.

"Did too," Helen replied. "You said, 'Shirley, you're kidding.'"

"Shirley?" I said. "No, no. I said *surely*."

"Are you sure?" Helen said, confused.

"Not anymore," I admitted.

Oh, brother. Now we were both confused. I scribbled in my journal: Witness saw mummy with shopping bag.

"Pretty strange," I said.

"I don't know *what's* stranger," Mila observed. "That Helen saw a mummy . . . or the conversation I just heard!"

Chapter Ten

Pumpkin Pie?

I never really believed it. I mean, it was fun to talk about mummies and all that. But I thought it was just talk — just my rotten brothers telling me crazy stories.

But now I didn't know what to think.

Did the mummy really rise from the dead? Was this his idea of Halloween fun? Stealing a bag of worms?

The trouble was, I didn't have enough facts. And you can't solve a mystery without facts. It's like trying to finish a jigsaw puzzle with a few pieces missing.

 290

Just not gonna happen.

"Maybe the worm thing wasn't such a hot idea," Mila said.

"Poor Joey," I said glumly. "It will break his heart. We sold tickets and everything."

Meanwhile, a group of kids was gathered around Helen.

"He's back," I heard Bobby Solofsky say. "The mummy has returned!"

That nearly sent the class into a panic. Ralphie Jordan told everyone about what happened to Twinkles the cat and Earl Bartholemew.

"And don't forget Mr. Reilly," Kim Lewis said. "His hair turned white when he saw the mummy."

The more kids talked, the more afraid they got. A few boys even hid in the closet until Ms. Gleason told them that enough was enough. She barked, "That's enough of this silliness."

Ms. Gleason stood up and slammed the

closet doors shut. Unfortunately, her tail got stuck between the doors. That made her even madder.

That's when Ms. Gleason saw that Geetha Nair was hiding under a desk.

"Geetha, what are you doing under there?"

"Hiding from the mummy," Geetha answered in a quivery voice.

Ms. Gleason heaved a heavy sigh. "Please come out, Geetha. I don't think mummies go to school."

Suddenly, Geetha pointed toward the door and screamed, "THEN WHAT'S HE DOING HERE?!"

Everyone stared at the door. A hand, wrapped in bandages, slowly pushed it open.

Kids screamed and dived under desks.

But I stood my ground. Not because I was brave. But because this particular mummy looked a little familiar.

"Oof," the mummy mumbled as he bumped into Ms. Gleason's desk.

"Joey?" I said. "Is that you?"

The mummy lifted a bandage and looked at me with one eye. "Hey, Jigsaw. Nice costume. It's me, Joey." He looked around the classroom. "Why is everyone under their desks? Did the hamsters get out again?"

I noticed that Joey was holding a bag. *My bag.* I snatched it from his hand. "I've been looking all over for this."

"Hey, don't get mad," Joey said. "Besides, I thought you said there were worms in there."

Bigs and Mila gathered around.

Joey continued, "See, I had been thinking about the worms all day. I was worried about them in that box of yours. So I thought I'd take them outside for a little exercise."

"Exercise?" I said.

"And fresh air," Joey added.

I scratched the back of my neck. "So what's the problem?" I asked.

Joey opened the bag and pulled out a box. It was shaped like my box. Except it was white, not gray. Joey opened the lid. "See for yourself."

I looked inside. "Pie?"

Joey stuck his thumb into the pie and gave it a lick. "Mmmm, pumpkin," he said.

Then I remembered what Ms. Gleason

had said. *She used the same kind of bag for her pie today.*

Mila must have been reading my mind. She said, "But if Joey took Ms. Gleason's pumpkin pie . . . then who has the worms?"

Chapter Eleven
Mila Saves the Day

I turned to Bigs. "Where were you just now, before you came into the classroom?"

Bigs jerked his thumb toward the door. "I delivered a bag for Ms. Gleason. It was for the —"

"— pumpkin pie contest!" Mila shouted, finishing his sentence.

Somehow the bags got switched. Joey took the pie by mistake. And Bigs delivered a box of worms!

Uh-oh.

There was no time to waste. "Bigs, Mila, let's go — and bring the pie!"

We raced to the auditorium.

The halls were crowded with ghouls and ghosts. We saw pirates and superheroes, ballerinas and princesses. We saw a giant M&M chatting with Pocahontas. We even saw a four-legged cow. With so much going on, no one paid much attention to a vampire, Frankenstein, and a wrestler hustling down the hall.

Bigs opened the auditorium door a crack.

"What do you see?" Mila asked.

Bigs whispered, "I see the principal, Mr. Rogers, standing in front of a long table. He has a fork in his hand."

"This isn't good," Mila said.

"He's already judging the pie contest," Bigs explained.

We all poked our heads through the crack in the door. Mr. Rogers placed a fork

in his mouth. He chewed thoughtfully. The school secretary, Mrs. Garcia, stood beside him. She wrote on a clipboard.

"Mr. Rogers is at the end of the table, Jigsaw," Bigs said. "He's opening the last box!"

"What can we do now?" Mila asked.

"WAIT!" I screamed.

But it was too late.

We ran up to the table. Mr. Rogers — who, by the way, was dressed like The Cat in the Hat — stared at us. Then down into the box. Then at us again.

He had found the worms.

And we were in big, big trouble.

Mr. Rogers's face turned red. "Is this some kind of foolish prank?" he demanded.

I stammered, "I . . . er . . . you see . . . ah . . ."

Mr. Rogers crossed his arms and stared down at me. "I'm waiting, Theodore."

Mila spoke up. "Great job, Mr. Rogers. You found Jigsaw's worms."

Mr. Rogers grimaced. "Apparently so."

"It's my mistake," Bigs piped up. He handed Mr. Rogers the bag with Ms. Gleason's pumpkin pie. "I brought the wrong bag."

"And these worms?" Mr. Rogers asked.

How could I ever explain it, I wondered.

Mila thought quick. "They're for Jigsaw's costume!" Mila reached into the box and

pulled out a worm. She placed it on my head.

Then Bigs grabbed a few and laid them on my shoulders.

"It adds to the overall creepiness," Mila explained.

Now it was Mr. Rogers's turn to stand in silence.

"Like in the poem," Mila said.

"Poem?"

"Yes, you know:

'The worms go in, the worms go out.
They crawl in your stomach
And out through your mouth.'"

Mr. Rogers rubbed his eyes and groaned.

"I'll get the aspirin," Mrs. Garcia offered.

"Yes, thank you, that would be nice," Mr. Rogers said to her. He turned back to us. "As for you three. Please get back to your classroom, it's nearly time for the parade. And I've got one more pie to taste."

We started to leave.

"Wait!" Mr. Rogers called out. "Please take the worms. Unless they are students here, they don't belong in school."

Chapter Twelve

Joey's Big Moment

The Halloween parade was a gigantic success. All the parents cheered and waved. Cameras flashed. Camcorders whirred. Both my parents were there . . . and so was Grams, waving wildly.

When we got back to room 201 after our march around the school, it was time for the class party. We ate spider cupcakes, opened treat bags, played games, and listened to music.

Everyone turned to look when Mr. Rogers burst through the door. Smiling happily, he handed Ms. Gleason a blue ribbon. She won first prize in the contest! We all clapped and cheered.

At long last, Ms. Gleason let us go outside for afternoon recess. Here was the moment we'd been waiting for.

Eddie Becker clapped Joey on the back. "Nearly everybody bought a ticket," he said. "We're going to be rich!"

We crowded into a tight circle. Joey selected a worm from the box. It was short but thick.

Joey looked at Bobby. "Show me the money," he said.

Mila made a face. "You couldn't pay me a million dollars to eat one of those things."

Ralphie Jordan volunteered. "For a million dollars," he said, "I'd eat a hundred of those suckers."

Bobby held out a portrait of George Washington. Joey reached for the money.

Bobby caught him by the wrist. "No swallowing it whole," he said. "I want to see you chew."

Lucy Hiller turned green.

Nicole Rodriguez turned away.

"Do it, Joey!" Mike Radcliffe urged.

"I need something to wash it down with," Joey Pignattano said. I was prepared for that. I handed Joey a juice box.

"Joey, don't!" Danika said. "That's a living creature."

Joey scratched his head. "It's just a worm," he replied.

 307

"So," Danika said. "Worms are people, too. That little guy has a mom and dad just like you. How do you think they'll feel when they find out that their son was eaten by a second-grader?"

"Who asked you, Danika?" Bobby shot back. "This is between Joey and me."

Danika shook her head sadly. "That little fella's probably got a name. Like Slimy or Slippy or something."

Joey poked at the worm with his finger. "Hi, Slippy," he said. "Are you ticklish?"

"Enough!" Bobby demanded. "Eat it or give my money back."

Joey looked at Danika. "Sorry," he said. "But this is business."

Joey opened his mouth. The worm dangled above his tongue.

And he ate it.

Three chews and a swallow.

He actually ate it.

I was right. It wasn't something you see every day. And that's probably a good thing.

Yuck!

After school, I split the dollar with Mila, fifty-fifty, and we went trick-or-treating around the neighborhood. We saw witches and ghosts, hoboes and tramps. But we didn't see any more mummies.

That was fine with me. I'd already seen enough for one day.

And as they say in the detective business . . . that *wraps* up another case for Jigsaw Jones!